ENEMIES AND EXPECTING

CLARE CONNELLY

PRESENTS

Recycling programs for this product may not exist in your area.

ISBN-13: 978-1-335-61405-6

Enemies and Expecting

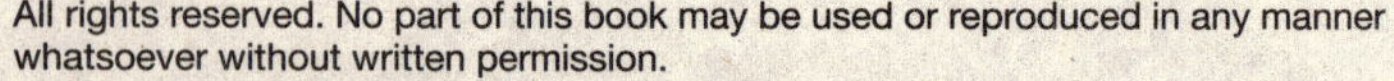

For questions and comments about the quality of this book, please contact us at CustomerService@Harlequin.com.

Harlequin Enterprises ULC
22 Adelaide St. West, 41st Floor
Toronto, Ontario M5H 4E3, Canada
www.Harlequin.com

HarperCollins Publishers
Macken House, 39/40 Mayor Street Upper,
Dublin 1, D01 C9W8, Ireland
www.HarperCollins.com

Printed in Lithuania

1 2 3 4 5 6 7 8 9 10 LIT 28 27 26 25

“Wait.” Rosie paced the gravel driveway, fingers pressed to her lips. “I can’t do this.”

Aristotle stood his ground, arms crossed over his chest. “Which part?”

“This.” She twisted her engagement ring. “All of it. The engagement. Marrying you. Telling them.” She looked anxiously toward the mansion. “Aristotle, this is a mistake.”

His lips pursed. “You’re pregnant with my baby. There is no alternative.”

“But surely we can—”

“I misspoke. There is one alternative,” he said, lifting a finger into the air, holding it between them.

She stopped walking and stared at him, her stomach in loops. “Court.”

He dipped his head once. “I have lawyers currently preparing our wedding documents, but if you’d prefer, I can brief them instead for a custody hearing.”

She felt the blood drain from her face. “Aristotle,” she whispered, tears springing to her eyes, surprising her. She blamed pregnancy hormones. She was under no illusions when it came to this man’s awful, hateful ways.

For the briefest moment, something shifted in his expression. Regret? Sympathy? Something soft. But then his features tightened into a mask of determination. “I will not have my child doubt my commitment to them.”

Clare Connelly was raised in small-town Australia among a family of avid readers. She spent much of her childhood up a tree, Harlequin book in hand. Clare is married to her own real-life hero, and they live in a bungalow near the sea with their two children. She is frequently found staring into space—a surefire sign she is in the world of her characters. She has a penchant for French food and ice-cold champagne, and Harlequin novels continue to be her favorite-ever books. Writing for Harlequin Presents is a long-held dream. Clare can be contacted via clareconnelly.com or on her Facebook page.

Books by Clare Connelly

Harlequin Presents

Pregnant Before the Proposal
Unwanted Royal Wife
Billion-Dollar Secret Between Them
Blackmail to White Veil
Greek's Ring of Redemption
Wedding Night Ultimatum

The Diamond Club

His Runaway Royal

Royally Tempted

Twins for His Majesty

A Greek Inheritance Game

Billion-Dollar Dating Deception
Tycoon's Terms of Engagement

Visit the Author Profile page at Harlequin.com for more titles.

ENEMIES AND EXPECTING

CHAPTER ONE

IN THE END, it turned out that no matter how many pep talks Rosie gave herself in the lead-up to this milestone birthday, nothing had adequately prepared her for coming face to face with her stepbrother four years after they'd stupidly fallen into bed together. Though 'fallen' was nowhere near the right verb, and come to think of it, there had been no bed either.

There'd been sparks, seduction, temptation and flame. Fire and heat. Her inexperience no match for the fact that from the moment her fourteen-year-old self had clapped eyes on Aristotle Machairas, she'd been his for a song—and for the first time in her life, at her chauffeur father's wedding to his billionaire mother, when she was twenty years old, Aristotle had finally looked at her and seen a woman. Or so she'd thought.

With his thick brown hair and eyes that were so dark one could easily get lost in their galactic depths, to the way his eyes were thickly rimmed with sweeping, long lashes—that was nothing to the incredible construction of his face. Where mere mortals were simply a hodge-podge of their forebears' DNA, Aristotle's face looked to have been lovingly carved by the most skilled master sculptor, with attention being paid to his square jaw, long straight nose, high cheekbones and a chin that somehow screamed arrogance despite the dimple in its centre. His jaw was almost always covered in stubble, which just added to his masculine allure.

An allure she wished she could feel a hell of a lot less of.

It had been four years, after all. Four years since that night—that had been, to borrow another's phrase, the best and worst of times. The best, in how his body had made hers feel. Despite it having been her first time—and the fact he wasn't aware of that beforehand—he was somehow so skilled that his swift invasion had barely hurt, because of how masterfully he'd stoked the fires of her need beforehand. And after that initial shock had worn off, the pleasure that had consumed her had been life-altering.

So too the coldness he'd displayed afterwards—the worst of times.

And then, there'd been the discovery that it had all been a dare, from his cruel friends.

Seduce the chauffeur's stupid daughter, who'd lusted after him from afar for years. She'd thought she'd kept her crush hidden, but apparently, his social circle had noticed, and thought it some great big joke. Memories of the things they'd said still haunted her. *'Not quite up to your usual standard... Scraping the bottom of the barrel isn't your usual style... At least she's got big breasts...'*

The next morning, he'd come to see her. To make sure she was 'okay'. Not because of the cruel dare—he hadn't known she'd heard his friends—but because it was her first time. How could she have answered that? Physically, she was fine. But emotionally, that was a whole other story.

Devastated, but determined not to show it, she'd presented him with an award-worthy act, as though she hadn't cared one way or another about losing her virginity.

She'd never been so happy to go back to her life in

England—a life she'd always hated because of her mother's coldness and vindictive rejection—heart battered and bruised, determined never to set eyes on the man again.

And now that she was here, all that hatred and rage was firing anew. *That*, she told herself comfortingly, was what she felt. Not desire. How could she, for that pig of a man?

Albeit a devastatingly handsome one. For beyond the perfection of his face was a body that was pure Adonis, as though he spent his life honing each muscle and sinew. She knew that was not the case. Aristotle Machairas had little time for vanity, or the gym. He'd taken over the family business after his father's death five years earlier, turning an already impressive investment company into a global powerhouse with the same strength one felt simply by looking at his physique. It simply emanated from him.

Bastard.

She'd managed to squirm out of any further trips to this ancient, sprawling estate in Filothei, a monied suburb on the outskirts of Athens. From its perch on the side of a hill, it boasted superb views down over the ancient city. Not to mention a tennis court, two swimming pools, a helipad, a seventeen-bedroom mansion and several guest houses, a ten-car garage, structured gardens as well as a wild forest that crept up to the edges of the estate as a constant reminder that nature was always there, waiting to untame what humans had done to the world. She knew better though. She knew though that some secrets could not be hidden—she'd dug deep into the earth to uncover them.

The first time Rosie had arrived here, she'd thought she'd died and gone to heaven. Her father's prior job had been driving for a diplomat, and when Rosie had come to Athens to visit him, he'd always taken a hotel room for them.

It had been nothing compared to this. Here, she'd been

a guest in his luxurious chauffeur's cottage, and at his then employer's instruction, Rosie had been free to explore the grounds and 'make herself at home'. *'I had only one child, and he is away so often, building his own life. It's what you want, of course, but I do get lonely. Kyrios Machairas works such long hours, you see. So, please, little darling, explore the house, read the books. Tell me if you'd like me to find some friends for you to play tennis with.'*

Even before her husband had passed away and there was any prospect of Melina Machairas becoming more to Rosie, the woman had been kindness personified.

Which made the harshness and cruelty of her son all the harder to understand.

It also meant that it was impossible for Rosie to miss her stepmother's sixtieth birthday. However, it became apparent startlingly quickly that the 'small family get-together' she'd been promised was a serious understatement. Her taxi—which she'd insisted on hailing rather than having a car sent for her—was still forming plumes of dust on the long, winding driveway when she became conscious of the lines of staff, dressed in suits, moving from the house and around the corner like ants who'd caught the hint of a picnic.

Pushing the sleeves of her pale yellow cardigan up to her elbows—it was so much warmer in Greece than it had been in London when she'd set out that morning—she left her small suitcase where it was and walked around the corner towards the formal gardens, where she very quickly saw that a large marquee had been set up for this evening's party. She hovered on the edge of a small courtyard, bordered on three sides by a large green hedge and on the final side by a high brick wall, behind which there was an old statue and a big wrought iron chair—she'd used to sit there and read books as a teenager, when she wanted privacy. She moved closer to the hedge, taking in the sweet fragrance of magnolia, as her eyes swept the activity a little way in the distance. There must have been a hundred staff members moving about, arranging tables, chairs, flowers, fridges.

She shook her head in bemusement as she turned with the intention of reclaiming her suitcase and finding her father, only to come breast to chest with the man she'd been dreading seeing since she'd stalked away from him four years earlier.

She was now twenty-four, he twenty-eight—but he looked exactly the same, and she *felt* exactly the same. Gauche and inexperienced, young and unwanted. Never mind that she'd given herself a serious image overhaul after that excruciating night, and the things his friends had said. Hair that had once been a brassy red had been toned down to a glorious cool auburn, and instead of keeping it short around her shoulders, she'd let it grow and form natural waves. Pale, milky skin was harder to change, but she'd learned to apply make-up that complemented her colouring, and to choose clothes that enhanced her complexion, as well as her shorter, curvy physique. She knew that she wasn't unattractive. Enough men hit on her to recognise that as fact. But compared to the exquisite beauty of Aristotle, she'd probably always feel like this.

Diminished.

Less than.

She knew her cheeks would be flushing pink—she could feel the heat building in them.

Furious with herself for acting like the awkward teen she'd been when they'd first met, and he'd arrived unexpectedly to find her sitting in the family room poring over an old collection of encyclopedias, she flicked her lips into something that could best be described as a terse smile and went to sidestep him without saying so much as a word.

She should have known better.

No sooner had she gained a hint of freedom than his voice emerged, halting her in her tracks.

'Rosemary, stop.'

She ground her teeth.

He'd always called her that, despite the fact she'd been 'Rosie' to everyone from birth.

'Why?' she asked, without turning around.

He came to stand in front of her, so her little gesture of defiance hardly seemed to matter.

He didn't say anything, at first. His eyes simply landed on her face then glided over her slowly, scanning her, studying her.

No doubt to report back to his horrible friends.

She was wearing a simple summer dress beneath her cardigan—hardly the dream outfit for this kind of confrontation. She'd planned on having time to shower and change into her party dress before seeing this man again.

'It's been a long time.' His voice was just as she remembered it, just as it had filled her dreams far more often than she cared to admit. That throaty, accented tone forever imprinted in her memory banks, able to be conjured up without any effort whatsoever.

Yet hearing it for real set her pulse alight in a way she bitterly resented. Her body seemed determined to betray her.

'Not long enough, in my opinion.'

'You are still angry.'

Her brain exploded. She opened her mouth to chew him out, to tell him that there was absolutely no statute of limitations for anger when someone treated you as coldly and cruelly as he had, but pride came to her rescue, reminding her that she had no intention of letting him know how much he'd hurt her.

'I'm not angry, Aristotle, I just don't have anything to say to you. We're not friends.'

'We're step-siblings,' he reminded her, his tone scathing, because they both knew they were no such thing. While they'd met when Rosie was fourteen and Aristotle eighteen, she'd simply been the daughter of the chauffeur. Their parents had married some six years later, when they were both well and truly adults in the world.

'We're strangers.'

'Who've slept together.'

She sucked in a sharp breath, surprised that he was willing to be so forthright about their experience.

'Did you think I'd forgotten?' she said, under her breath. And then, more loudly, for his benefit, 'So what? That was a thousand years ago—'

'Four years,' he ground out.

'And it meant nothing,' she finished.

'Obviously.'

Obviously. Because how could it? How could a gorgeous, sexy, experienced billionaire like Aristotle, who routinely dated stunning heiresses slash Instagram influencers, ever look at someone like Rosie and be genuinely attracted?

Mortification threatened to curl her toes, but she held her ground, her face a study in defiance. 'Is that all?'

'No.'

Her pulse fired up. Just being close to him set every cell in her body alight.

'We need to talk about what happened.'

She felt herself blanch. 'I beg your pardon, we absolutely don't.'

His jaw clenched visibly, eyes going from dark to black. 'Our parents have no idea about that night.'

'Of course they don't. I was hardly going to shout it from the rooftops.'

'Nor was I.'

Yeah, no kidding. As if he'd boast about seducing someone like her.

'So? Let's chalk it up to the biggest mistake of our lives and move on,' she suggested firmly, going to sidestep him once more. But this time, with a sharp exhalation of frustration, he reached out and curled his fingers around her wrist, drawing her to an immediate stop. It felt as though he'd poured a whole city power grid's worth of electricity into her veins in one fell swoop. So much charge sparked in her veins she saw stars in her eyes.

'Don't touch me.'

To her disappointment, he let her go.

'For my mother's sake, we have to act as though we are—'

She waited, lips pursed in a mask of mock impatience, when in reality, there was something borderline hypnotic about being close to him again.

'At least tolerant of one another.'

'I don't intend on spending enough time with you for your mother or my father to form any opinion on us whatsoever.'

His jaw tightened at the mention of her father, and she understood why. He didn't approve of how quickly they'd married, after his father's death. She didn't completely blame him for that—the timing had surprised her, too.

'You think we're not going to be thrown together at this damned event?'

'Nice,' she muttered. 'It's your mother's birthday.'

His expression shifted into a scowl. 'I'm aware. And she

is no doubt going to want photographs of the "happy family". Particularly given you've been absent so long.'

'Well, whose fault is that?' she snapped, then immediately wished she hadn't, because it somehow yielded too much power to him. She tried to reverse the damage with a flippant roll of her eyes. 'Anyway, I'm sure your mother has bigger things to think about than you and me.'

'There is no you and me.' His voice was sharp, a fierce rejection.

She ignored the familiar emotional bruise in the centre of her chest—the sense that the last thing he could ever want was to have anything more to do with her.

'No kidding.'

'But for my mother, we should work on at least pretending to be civil to one another.'

'You wouldn't know civility if it came and bit you on the—'

He moved quickly, pressing a finger to her lips, startling her body with that same mega-dump of electrical current. 'You should be careful, *mikroúla*. The more you taunt me, the more I am tempted to show what a liar you are.'

Heat flooded her cheeks, and her eyes dashed frantically behind him, to the staff. They were far away though, and obscured by the hedge of the courtyard.

'You think I'm lying when I point out that you are rude, and unpleasant and—'

'And yet you fell apart in my arms,' he said smoothly, surprising her then by wrapping an arm around her waist and yanking her against his big, strong body, his hard, firm planes making her mouth go all dry and dusty.

'Yeah, well, I didn't know what I was doing, obviously,' she said, in a valiant attempt at bravado that came out shaky.

'So you're saying it was just your inexperience?'

'What else explains it?'

He pulled on her again, pressing her tighter to his body. All the breath seemed to leave her lungs. She felt weak at the knees and her stomach flipped as though it had developed an inbuilt trampoline.

'You might not like me, Rosemary, but you have always wanted me, haven't you?' he asked, in a voice that sounded serious but couldn't help but be interpreted as anything other than a massive flex. Because yes. She'd always wanted him. As a lovestruck teenager, then when she'd come back for her father's wedding, thinking she'd finally grown into the kind of woman he might look at, she'd learned it had all been a cruel dare.

Her stomach went from flipping to tightening with knots. 'We should focus on the first part of that statement. I don't like you. No, I *hate* you,' she spat. 'And everyone like you.'

Her insult didn't appear close to hitting the mark. If anything, he just looked more determined. More dangerously, darkly handsome.

'Is that so?' he asked, his head swooping down suddenly so he could kiss her, hard and fast, his mouth claiming hers as though the whole world's survival depended on it. It was a kiss that knocked every bit of sense and fight from her, knocked everything like control, rational thought and reason totally from her mind. A kiss so much like their last first kiss, a kiss that had fundamentally and swiftly reshaped everything she thought she knew about the world, so all she could do was surrender to it completely.

'Then tell me to stop,' he challenged, pulling up to stare into her eyes. 'Tell me to stop,' he repeated, taking a step forward and propelling her with him, and then another step, guiding them around the corner, behind the tall wall, without breaking eye contact. He spun her then, so her back connected with the bricks, the surface cool despite the heat of the day. Here, in the shade of the house, it was saved from the Greek sun. Another reason she—and her pale English skin—had liked this hiding spot so much.

'Well, Rosemary? What's it to be?'

She glared up at him, searching for something pithy to say, something withering and insulting. Any one of the epithets that had been flying around her head for years, in response to how he viewed her, the way he'd treated her that night.

'Oh, go to hell,' was all she could get out. And the effect of the words was entirely ruined by the way her hand reached up and curled in the fabric of his shirt, holding on as if for dear life.

'I have no doubt that I will,' was his short response, before he dropped his head once more, claiming her mouth with his. Now, shielded completely from even an accidental view, he didn't hold back. His hands roamed her body as though he were a starving man finally brought to food, running over her fast and desperately, mapping her, tracing her, in a way that was so thorough there was no room to feel self-conscious about the curves that were undoubtedly the polar opposite of his usual conquest.

Stop this, a voice of reason cautioned as she moaned softly, deep in her throat.

When he swore in his native tongue, she felt it spread through her whole body, lighting fires in places she hadn't known she possessed. It was a curse, and a calling, a seeking of her response, so suddenly her hands were roaming his body with every bit as much desperation as his own, pushing his shirt from his jeans so her fingertips could connect with warm, bare flesh, running over him in the same frenzied state he was employing, until they were both breathing hard in between kisses.

His mouth then was roaming to her jaw, kissing her there, his stubble hard, his mouth demanding, and his hands were pushing her skirt up, so his fingers could cup her bottom, pressing her against his unmistakable hardness, his arousal pressing to her sex so she whimpered low in her throat, the plea swirling around and around in her mouth before finally ejecting on a final cry. He pulled up then, eyes finding hers, latching to them.

If she was going to pull back from the brink, this would have been the moment, for in his gaze there was an unspoken question: a need to confirm she meant what she said. She simply tilted her head back and stared at the bright blue sky overhead, her body flushed from head to toe. It was madness. A wild, utter surrender to a state of abandon, but that didn't matter. Because for all she understood that, she also knew that if she didn't give into this, she would live to regret it.

It had been four years, and she'd spent every day since then hating and avoiding him. But here, now, nothing mattered more than giving her body what it clearly sought, to hell with what came next.

Except there would be no 'next'. This was as meaningless to him as it had been four years earlier.

For all she knew, this was another sick dare from his stupid friends. So what? Did that matter, when she was also getting what she wanted? And so much better this time, because her eyes were wide open. She no longer had any fantasies about Aristotle being some tall, dark and handsome romantic hero. He was an arrogant bastard, but he was also very, very good at the whole sex thing. She had no intention of cutting off her nose to spite her face… It had been four years since their first time, after all, and in the intervening years she'd only dated two men, neither of whom had managed to set her soul on fire.

'Take me, Aristotle,' she demanded, getting a thrill out of the rawness of her request. 'Take me, here, now, and then leave me the hell alone.'

He pulled away from her, eyes glittering darkly. 'That sounds like an excellent idea.'

A second later, he was unfastening his jeans, pulling himself from the confines of his boxer briefs and deftly removing her underwear at the same time. It was all so fast, so desperate. Then, with the same hungry speed, he lifted her easily, wrapping her legs around his waist in the same moment he drove into her, making her see stars, heaven, God, the entire formation of the universe in Technicolor sparkles.

Everything glowed, everything shimmered. Pleasure tore her apart and there was no way Rosie had it in her to care.

It was the last thing he'd expected to happen.

And, quite possibly, the worst. Rosemary Richardson was a thorn in his side and little more, yet within minutes of her arrival he'd taken her, hard, fast, desperately, against the cold brick of the courtyard. Taken her as though he'd been thinking about it nonstop for the last four years, when the opposite was true. He hadn't thought about Rosemary at all, except to be grateful she'd made herself scarce.

He hadn't *wanted* to think about her, or that night when he'd slept with her, and discovered that she was a twenty-year-old virgin. All softly sweet and responsive, calling his name out in a way that had turned parts of him to liquid.

She was *not* his type, and he'd been damned stupid to forget that.

Yet here he was, four years later, and he'd done the same stupid thing.

Worse, he hadn't used a condom.

The thought speared him in the side for a frantic moment, because of all the things he knew about himself, the fact he didn't want children—ever—was one of them.

'*Christós*,' he groaned, pulling out of her and placing her down, voice more accusing than he'd intended. His body protested at his swift withdrawal, craving more of her. 'I didn't use protection.' He cursed again, the word dragged from deep in his gut.

Her eyes widened and her hands, trembling slightly, lifted to her delicate face. Her beautiful face, he thought, before he could stifle the thought. But it was true. There had always been something charming about Rosemary. Even as the fourteen-year-old who'd first arrived, she'd had an innate grace and wisdom in her features and the watchfulness of her gaze.

But it was at twenty that she'd really started to show what a stunner she was, with that flawless complexion, wideset green eyes, dainty freckles across her nose and full, pouty pink lips. She had dimples in both cheeks when she smiled and a figure that was curvy in all the places he found most tempting. Breasts, hips, butt, she was some kind of ancient sculpture brought to life, and his hands seemed to develop a mind of their own when he touched her, so he grabbed every bit of her and squeezed, felt, committed to memory.

'I'm on the pill,' she said, her throat shifting as she swallowed.

'Thank God,' he spat quickly, so her gaze narrowed a little and her features tightened, visibly rejecting him.

'Oh, yes, heaven forbid you should have a baby with someone like me.' She shoved at his chest then, and he was in such a state of shock from the realisation that he'd forgotten such a basic requirement of sex that he stepped backwards. 'What would anyone think?'

'It's not about you,' he corrected with the appearance of calm as he fastened his jeans back up, wincing a little at the way his cock fought the restriction.

'It feels a little about me.'

'I don't want children,' he said flatly. 'Let alone in circumstances such as this.'

'Yeah, well, that makes two of us. I can't think of anything worse than carrying *your* baby, in particular.'

He ignored the brief, uncharacteristic flash of feeling that her statement caused. An immediate image of her growing round with his baby, of him having a baby at all. Despite the knowledge that he would never procreate, he couldn't help but feel some ancient stirring of *something* when he contemplated the primal drive to reproduce. The anchor point he'd lost at fifteen?

'Now, if you'll excuse me, I want to go and see my father.'

She turned to stalk away but he reached for her on autopilot, not wanting to leave it like this. Or perhaps not wanting her to leave at all.

She spun around, lips quivering in a way that pulled at every fibre of decency he possessed—albeit buried deep inside his chest.

'No one can know about this,' he said, earning another flicker of her eyes, a look of hurt in their depths he couldn't fail to read.

'So you've said.' She jerked her hand free, and he allowed it. 'God, I really do hate you.'

CHAPTER TWO

Four months later

'You've been in London, you say?' Melina Machairas asked down the phone line.

It was early enough that the sky was still tinged with darkness, with a hint of dawn colours spreading like fingertips across the horizon—streaks of pink, purple, a splash of gold.

'I'm still in London,' he corrected.

She made a considering noise. 'What for?'

'Investor meetings.'

Another noise—one he knew well. His mother was scheming.

'Whatever it is you are thinking, say it.' He leaned back in his chair, reaching for his thick, dark coffee in the same movement.

'How do you know I'm thinking anything?'

'Because I know you.' She might not have been his biological mother—something he'd become shockingly, painfully aware of at the age of fifteen, but she was still the woman who'd raised him. Every nuance of hers was familiar to him.

'I don't suppose you've seen Rosie?'

He closed his eyes against the question—and, more accurately, the unwelcome impact it had on his body. The way his gut tightened and his cock surged with a rush of blood. Damn that woman. Damn her sweet vanilla fragrance and long, curling hair that was the most striking colour he'd ever seen.

'You know we do not socialize.'

His mother sighed. 'Yes, I just thought perhaps at one of your fundraisers or events…'

He flattened his lips. Rosemary and he moved in very different circles. Up until her father's marriage to his mother, Rosemary and Glen Richardson had hardly been the kind of people that would wind up at the social occasions he frequented.

Rosemary still wasn't.

He knew—because it was impossible not to glean certain things about her—that she was a junior archaeologist, often posted in strange, out-of-the-way locations. He had no idea how she juggled that with her fair skin, and yet, remembering the way she'd pored over those Britannicas, her job choice did make sense.

'Do you think you could check on her?'

He instantly rejected the idea, but at least managed to stop the harsh 'no' from flying out of his mouth. 'Why? Rosemary undoubtedly has plenty of friends—I doubt she needs me.'

His mother lowered her voice. 'We're worried about her. We've been trying to get her to come home, but she's refusing.'

He ignored the anger that flared inside of him at his mother's use of the word 'home'. Rosemary was an outsider, just as her father was.

He could only thank God his mother had listened to common sense and had Glen sign an ironclad prenuptial agreement before the wedding. Meaning that while he might enjoy the benefits of a billionaire's lifestyle for now, it was entirely temporary.

'Rosemary is a big girl. I'm sure she can take care of herself.'

His mother made a sound of frustration. 'It's been hard on her, being excluded from the dig. She's missing fieldwork, and has no idea when she'll be able to get back to it. Certainly not for a year at least, but even then, she can hardly drag a baby around the world—'

He sat up straighter, as though a blade of lightning had cracked against the side of his skull.

'Did you say "baby"?'

His mother sighed again. 'Honestly, do you ever check your WhatsApp?'

He pulled his phone from his ear, quickly flicking into the messaging app. 'There's nothing there.'

'Oh. I thought I sent something. I don't know. I'm so useless with technology, Aristotle.' There was a shuffling noise, but Aristotle barely heard it. The word 'baby' was flying around and around his mind, setting parts of him on fire, turning others to ice. 'You'll have to teach me, next time you're here.'

His lips compressed tighter. 'Are you telling me Rosemary Richardson is pregnant?'

'Your stepsister, Rosie, yes, darling.'

He gripped his phone so tightly it was a surprise it didn't pop out of his hand. 'And who, may I ask, is the father?'

'That's the thing. She won't say. I know she was dating someone a few months ago. Some historian or researcher, someone she met through work. Do you think you could go and check in on her? Take her some dinner or something? Let her know she has family if she needs us.'

His head was pounding all of a sudden, as though his

brain had begun to beat and throb, to expand so hard and fast against the confines of his skull that it hurt all over.

'Of course,' he said darkly, brow beading in a hint of perspiration as he stood and reached for his suit jacket. 'What is her address?'

Despite the fact he spent several months a year in London for work, he had no clue where his 'stepsister' lived—a fact he'd always been glad of. Until now. He took down her address and then said silkily, 'You'd better give me her phone number, too.'

Because there was no way he was going to let Rosemary get away from him. If there was any chance she was pregnant with his baby, he needed to know.

But just the thought of it threatened to send him into an unwelcome state of panic, so he found himself clinging to what his mother had said—that Rosemary had been dating someone else around the time of her party. At least that cast some doubt on things. Surely that other man was more likely to be the father?

He ignored the pang of something darkly disapproving that flared at the thought of Rosemary sleeping with other men. Of course she had—and so she should have. If anything, he was the one who'd been in the wrong, the one who'd yet again taken advantage of the strangely alluring chemistry that sparked between them whenever they were together.

There were four years between them, but that might have been a decade when it came to life experience and outlook. Even now, at twenty-four, there was something startlingly sheltered about Rosie, something young and innocent.

His entire focus on the drive across town, to the Putney address his mother had given him, was on discounting the possibility of his being the father of her baby. The certainty that he just needed to see Rosemary, and have her confirm that, so he'd be able to go back to his own life, heaving a huge sigh of relief.

Up until a month ago, Rosie wouldn't have had any idea she was pregnant. There had been a few niggling symptoms, but nothing she'd paid much attention to. It was only a routine blood test, prior to heading deep into Colombia, that had revealed her pregnancy. Testing for it was a standard precaution, given the risk of Zika virus in the next dig location.

She hadn't batted so much as an eyelid at the pathology form, but when the results came back positive she could have been knocked over with a feather.

Pregnant!

She'd had four weeks to come to terms with the concept of having a baby, with the identity of the baby's father, and the impact it would have on her career. It was as if one sledgehammer after another was being slammed into her life, splintering every single part of it to shreds.

Telling her father and stepmother had been the hardest part because she'd known it would eventually lead to them telling Aristotle, but she could hardly keep such a thing as a pregnancy secret. And the baby? She'd agonized over that. This dear little lifeform, to whom she already felt so connected, was part Aristotle. On the one hand, her first instinct was to tell him. Of course! How could she not? But then, when she remembered the way he'd so vehemently insisted he never wanted children, his general coldness towards her—and everyone—she rejected the idea outright. It would be so much better for their baby to have one parent who loved them fully, rather than suffering the pain of a parent who couldn't open their heart. She knew that pain all too well.

She could only thank every deity known to man that she'd told her father a fib at Melina's birthday party, inventing some fictional work colleague boyfriend, to cover any hint of suspicion that might arise around her and Aristotle.

Not that he'd so much as looked at her for the rest of the night.

For all of his 'we should be civil' talk, he'd basically acted as though she didn't exist.

Which had suited her *fine.*

She turned her attention back to the research notes she was compiling for one of the on-field teams, ignoring the pang of jealousy in the centre of her chest. What she wouldn't give to be out there, doing the actual work. The thrill of discovery, the patience it took to sift sand and dirt, segment by segment, tracking every minor discovery, gently uncovering the secrets of the past. She'd always loved puzzles, and she'd always adored history: archaeology was the perfect combination of both.

And now it was a distant pipe dream.

Her door buzzer sounded and she cast it an exasperated glance, before remembering she was expecting some slides to be couriered over so she could categorise them. She stood, rubbing a hand over her very gently rounded stomach out of habit, her heart giving a little kick as she connected with the tiny life in there, and sighed.

For all it was a major mistake, and had the potential for disaster, at the same time she had felt instantly bonded with her little hitchhiker, the life forming inside of her. Bonded, and in love with. Utterly and completely.

She pasted a smile on her face and wrenched the door in, preparing to take the envelope of slides right up until the moment her gaze connected with Aristotle Machairas's and another sledgehammer slammed into her life.

This was an invasion of every single sense. It was a shocking crossing of the lines they'd implicitly formed. He *did not* invade her London life. This was her space. Her zone.

He was outside of it.

'We need to talk,' he said darkly, not waiting to be invited in. His big, broad frame brushed past her and he stalked into her small studio apartment, with the neat double bed, table and two chairs and kitchenette.

'This is where you live?' he demanded, nostrils flaring.

'Yeah, well, we aren't all born into squillion-dollar fortunes,' she said, ignoring her baby's claim on that fortune. Ignoring everything except her survival instinct. She closed the door gingerly, but stayed where she was—as far as she could possibly get from him.

He slammed his hands onto his hips, drawing attention to his slim waist, so her pulse became all thready and weak. She glowered at him rather than show any hint of attraction.

'I just had a very interesting conversation with my mother,' he said, voice measured, and yet she felt the emotion throbbing just beneath the surface and knew he was holding on by a thread.

'Oh?' she asked, still being careful, in the very faint hope that maybe, just maybe, something else might have brought him here in this enraged state.

'Is it mine?'

Hope died a swift death. She closed her eyes on a wave of agony and desperation.

Deny it. Tell him it's the fictional boyfriend's. Save yourself this conversation.

She opened her mouth, half intending to do just that, but the words died inside her throat.

'I should warn you, I will drag you to a doctor for a

DNA test so fast your head will spin, if you even think of lying to me.'

Her jaw dropped. 'You can't order me to take a damned test.'

'Care to test that theory?'

She felt the colour drain from her face.

'Is it mine?' he ground out, each word carefully enunciated so she flinched.

'Yes,' she whispered, closing her eyes as she pressed her back to the door and let it take her weight, needing the support.

He swore curtly. 'Are you sure?'

She nodded.

'My mother said you were seeing someone else around the same time.'

Her eyes blinked open to meet his. 'I made that up.'

He arched a brow. 'Or is it that you figure I'm worth more?'

It was such a vile thing to accuse her of that she could barely comprehend what he was suggesting.

'If I wanted your money,' she said slowly, with great dignity, 'I would have told you about this myself. Honestly, my biggest hope was that you'd never find out.'

'Hardly likely, all things considered.'

'Well, I went four years without having to see you. I was pretty sure I could go at least four more.'

'And then what, Rosemary? Introduce me to my son or daughter, a child almost old enough to be off to school?'

She tamped down on the panic his words brought.

'Why would you lie about a relationship?'

'Why do you think?' she demanded, storming closer towards him, then regretting it instantly when she caught a hint of his aftershave and her stomach began to somersault.

'I didn't want them to suspect anything had happened between us.'

His eyes narrowed, as if appraising that for the likelihood of truth. 'Why would they?'

'Good question. I guess I was just covering the bases.'

'So you're pregnant.'

It was a statement rather than a question, but she nodded slowly.

'And you're keeping the baby?'

She blanched at that. Strangely, given how disastrous this was for her professionally, she hadn't once considered *not* going through with it.

'Yes—' she tilted her chin defiantly '—but that doesn't matter. To you, I mean.'

He was perfectly still—so still, the air around him almost seemed to vibrate. 'I see. Tell me more.'

She felt a flicker of uncertainty. A presentiment of danger. But she ignored it. Whatever else he was, this man was, ostensibly, her stepbrother. She shuddered at that, though, because he wasn't. They were nothing like 'family'. The fact that their parents had married didn't make a single bit of difference to them.

'Obviously, you don't have to be involved at all. In fact, I'd prefer it that way. It's better if your mother and my father don't know that you're the dad.'

He nodded calmly, but there was something in his eyes that might have served as a warning if she'd been paying more attention.

'So you're planning to raise our baby here?' He gestured around the room, his arm only perhaps a metre or so from the wall at any given point. She followed his gesture with her gaze, then returned her attention to his face.

'As I said, you don't have to worry about that. This is my baby, not "our" baby. You're off the hook.'

'The facts would indicate otherwise.'

A *frisson* ran the length of her spine as she realised that this wasn't going exactly as she'd planned.

'You are pregnant with my child, yes?'

'Well, yes, but I know how you feel about it. You don't want children. You told me as much very, very clearly.'

'And you told me you were on the pill. Evidently, we were both wrong.'

Her brain struggled to compute his statement. 'I *was* on the pill,' she contradicted fiercely. 'It's not one hundred per cent foolproof.'

Dark colour slashed his cheeks.

'Are you saying that you were wrong about wanting children? That deep down you have some fantasy notion of being an amazing dad, or whatever?' She didn't give him a chance to answer. 'Because if that's true, fine. Go forth and breed. Just don't expect to be a part of our lives.' She pressed her palm to her stomach, drawing strength from the little lifeform.

But it was a mistake, because his eyes dropped to the gesture, landing on her stomach as his features lost the mask of cool control and showed, oh, so briefly, a surge of emotion.

'I do not want children,' he responded finally, drawing his gaze slowly back to her face and walking towards her with the same predatory stride. 'But it is no longer an academic question. You are pregnant with my child. The choice has been taken away from me.'

'As it was from me,' she hissed. 'Do you think this is my dream?' She flushed to the roots of her hair and wished she could recall the words. Even though her baby was still little more than a collection of cells, she couldn't bear the thought of them hearing her say any such thing. She lowered her voice to a whisper. 'I've lost my career, Aristotle. I can't go out in the field; I can't bring a baby around with me. At least, not easily, not to the locations I go,' she amended, thinking of the list she'd started to compile of 'safe' sites that might prove possible. But she'd need help, and who would offer it? Her mother was busy with her own life, her father in his. She had no siblings, and she could hardly ask a friend to take time off work to come with her for months at a time, accompanying her to locations that were often remote and dangerous, so she could continue working. Worse, could she bring her child to those places, many of them either war-torn or facing other threats?

She chewed on her lower lip as she felt the closing down of every single option like a physical pain.

'I'm aware of that.'

She concentrated hard on bringing herself back into the present conversation, even when her wheels were spinning and nothing was making much sense whatsoever.

'So let me help you.'

Her eyes widened. 'Don't you think you've done enough?'

His expression shifted slightly, showing for a moment the ruthless control for which he was famed. A shiver ran the length of her spine as she shook her head, moving as far away from him as she could get in the meagre apartment. It was a small studio, but it was private. Besides, she was on the road so much, she hardly needed more.

'I should have used a condom, you're right. I have never forgotten. Not once.'

She gripped the back of a chair tightly. The bond she felt with their baby refused to let her agree with him.

'I didn't think of it either,' she pointed out. Surprised that, even in this moment, she was willing to give him that cover.

But it was true. She had no antiquated feeling that contraception remained the man's job to sort out. She'd known damn well what they were doing, what she'd asked him to do, and the thought of a condom had been nowhere in her mind.

'It's done. Now we have to face the consequences of that.'

She swallowed past an unwelcome lump in her throat. 'I told you; I don't want anything from you. Not money, not time, not support. I'll work this out.'

'How?'

She closed her eyes, floundering. 'I don't know just yet.' Then, rallying, because she knew she had to at least appear strong, even when she didn't feel it, 'But it doesn't matter. It's my problem to solve.'

'You are pregnant with my baby,' he said slowly. 'I cannot ignore that fact.'

'But you *can*,' she pointed out. 'No one knows about us. Believe me, no one will suspect the great Aristotle Machairas is the father.'

His eyes narrowed.

'You can go on living your life as though this never happened. Please, Aristotle. You don't have to worry about this.'

'I'm not making myself clear,' he said, moving towards her in a few short paces. 'I have never wanted children. I have always taken great pains—until that afternoon—to ensure something like this couldn't happen. But you are pregnant; the baby is mine. And so there's nothing for it. We'll have to get married.'

Her jaw dropped and her ears started to ring as though they were filled with hummingbirds. 'What?'

'I'll organise everything. Obviously, the quicker the better.'

She stared at him, still unable to speak.

'Once we're married, you'll move in with me.'

She made some kind of incomprehensible noise.

'There will be a prenuptial agreement, much like your father signed.'

Her gaze narrowed. 'I'm not interested in your money, and I'm sure as hell not interested in marrying you.'

He nodded slowly, as though he was considering that, his face a study in reasonableness. 'And yet I presume, like me, you'd like to avoid a protracted court battle.'

Her heart twisted. 'Court battle?'

'For custody.'

'Custody,' she repeated, feeling like a parrot and not caring, pressing both hands to her stomach, pain lancing her. Scarring, horrible memories that she kept under firm lock and key—of her parents' awful, acrimonious divorce, the way she'd been turned into a pawn by her mother—made her feel raw all over. She trembled from the force of that trauma, from the ache he so easily, unknowingly invoked. She would *never* subject her child to that. Naively, perhaps, she'd presumed it would be a non-issue, given the fact Aristotle was her baby's father and he was about as paternal as a lump of wood.

'You cannot seriously think I would let you raise my child alone? And here, of all places?'

She stared at him, completely aghast. No, worse. She felt as though she'd been put into a spin-dryer and was rotating at high speed. Gravity had taken on a whole new meaning; she couldn't find anything solid to grab hold of.

'Wait, what?' She looked around. 'My apartment's fine, and obviously I'll get something bigger, at some point. When we need it.' The 'we' was protective. A reminder to both of them that she and the baby were already their own little team.

His nostrils flared. 'I don't mean your apartment. I mean London.'

He stared at her long and hard, his features taking on an expression she'd never before seen on him.

'Whatever else happens, this child will be raised as my son or daughter, in Greece. If you wish to be a part of their life, then accept my proposal. Otherwise? Get ready for court.'

CHAPTER THREE

FROM THE MOMENT he'd heard about her pregnancy he'd known that if the baby was his he would propose marriage. What choice did he have?

Discovering his adoption had split his soul in two. Every foundation of his life had been shaken. He'd learned that his own biological parents—whoever they were—hadn't wanted him. Hadn't loved him. That on some level he had been rejected by people who should have moved heaven and earth for him. It had changed him on every level. He had always been determined and driven, but overnight he'd shut everyone out. Already enrolled at boarding school, he'd stopped coming home for the holidays. He'd travelled with casual friends instead, choosing those superficial relationships rather than the lie that was his family home.

Parents who had raised him to believe he was a Machairas. It was all fake.

It was also a foundation of his character. Whatever he might have been like, had he not learned the truth, a part of him had died that fateful day and left in place of that one version of Aristotle another entirely. This one cold, with a heart that was entirely withdrawn. Bitten by the reality of his circumstances, the fact he was an outsider, he had made an artform of avoiding his parents.

Then he'd gone home one year, when he was eighteen, and Rosemary had been there, ensconced as though she'd always lived on the estate, and he'd felt strangely jealous. Replaced and usurped. Because he had never really belonged; it wasn't his home any more than it was hers.

He'd confronted his father once, after stumbling upon the court ruling pertaining to his adoption completely by accident, and the truth had been confirmed. They couldn't have children of their own, and so had adopted Aristotle. They knew nothing of his birth parents, his father had said: they hadn't wanted to know. Aristotle was theirs, from the moment they'd signed the documents. His father was, if anything, impatient with the conversation. They had never intended for Aristotle to know because it wasn't relevant. He was a Machairas, because they said so. Aristotle was forbidden from speaking to his mother about it.

For Aristotle, it had only served to stretch the black hole inside of him further, so that all the parts of him he'd once known were swallowed into its infinitesimal depths.

It was no surprise to Aristotle that his reaction to the pregnancy news had been one of visceral certainty.

His child would *never* doubt his or her place in his life. His child would know that he had fought for them, would know that they were wanted, valued. Even when he had no idea how to show that.

Even when it meant marrying Rosemary Richardson, the one woman he wanted to keep at a distance.

The one woman who seemed to destroy whatever grasp he had on his control. Twice now, she'd driven him over the edge of reason so he'd acted in a way that was deeply out of character.

'Seriously? Get the hell out of my home!' she shouted, dragging him back to the present with a thud.

He crossed his arms over his chest, staring down at her, ignoring the pang of guilt he felt at her obvious distress. What choice did he have? Since he was a teenager, he'd lived with a sense of abandonment and confusion, a feeling that he didn't know who he was or where he belonged. There was not a chance in hell he'd risk that happening to his own child. Rosemary's discomfort was unfortunate, but not his primary concern. Besides, she'd clearly intended to hide the truth of this situation from him, and their parents, which somewhat justified his overbearing approach—at least, in Aristotle's mind, in that moment.

'We need to have this discussion.'

'But we're not having a discussion!' She laughed almost manically. 'You're riding roughshod over everything I say, coming in here like some pregnancy dictator, demanding I marry you! It's the twenty-first century, Aristotle. You can be in the baby's life to some extent, without dragging me down the aisle.'

In the very back of his mind, he felt a flash of something like amusement. He knew he was considered an 'eligible bachelor'. That his fortune was eye-watering enough to make a lot of women willing to ignore the fact he was intentionally emotionally unavailable. What did intimacy matter when there was a never-ending credit card balance in the offing?

He ground his jaw, pushing the thoughts aside. He knew they weren't entirely fair. Not in this instance, at least.

Rosemary was—clearly—not looking for money, or she would have been the one to approach him with this news. She would have held it over his head to barter for whatever she wanted, not hidden away in this Putney bedsit. She certainly wouldn't be standing there with her pouty lips pursed and her eyes flashing daggers in his direction because he was offering to marry her. No, insisting on it.

'Let's think about our parents,' he said, trying a different tack. He knew how close she was, not only to her father, but to his mother as well. Their bond was obvious to anyone who observed them together.

And no wonder. His mother had been starved of affection from him ever since he'd learned the truth of his adoption. If he were a better man, he'd have been glad that she'd found it in the form of her relationship with Rosemary.

'I'd rather not.'

'Because you know how this will affect them.'

'They don't need to know,' she pleaded, her voice higher in pitch than usual.

He shook his head and, despite his best efforts, his voice came out with a hint of condescension. 'You're not thinking clearly. Life is long. Are you seriously going to hide the truth of our child's parentage from them?'

She twisted her fingers so sharply in front of her stomach he thought they might fall off. 'I…yes.'

'No,' he admonished immediately. 'For one thing, what if the child looks like me?'

Her eyes widened and her hands went from writhing themselves into knots to both pressing to her stomach, as though she could somehow stem that betrayal.

'We can cross that bridge when and if we get to it. Besides, you're not a lot like your parents, beyond your complexion. I'm nothing like my father.'

He shouldn't have been surprised by the way her words seemed to slice through him as daggers might have, but they were so unexpectedly frank, calling out something he'd known for years and dismissed, up until that fateful afternoon when he'd found the court ruling detailing his adoption, quite by accident.

'We are not lying to them about this.'

Her jaw clenched visibly. 'Since when are you such a stickler for the truth?'

He had absolutely no idea what she was talking about. If there was one character trait that could be reliably ascribed to him, it was that of honesty. Though, he supposed, with Rosemary, their interactions had been necessarily kept from his mother and her father.

'You have two choices, Rosemary. Marry me, or prepare for a fight.'

He hardened himself against sympathy when he saw the way she blanched and reached behind her for a chair to collapse into. Her eyes though stayed hooked to his, anger and accusation in their depths.

'I despise you.'

He ignored the way that sparked something in his gut. Something that made him want to reason with her, to apologise. He was doing what he had to, to show his child that they were loved and wanted, to avoid the rejection he'd known for so much of his life.

'Be that as it may, we're having a baby.'

He stood there watching her, studying her, waiting as she squeezed her eyes shut then dipped her head.

'I know.'

'So, what's it to be?'

She glanced up at him, her expression showing sheer mutinous rage. 'What do you think, you son-of-a-bitch? Obviously, given the options, I'll marry you.' And then, with a spirit that seemed to come from nowhere, like a phoenix rising from the ashes of her shock, she stood, closing the distance between them and jabbing a finger at his chest. 'But make no mistake about it: I will never forgive you for this.'

Beyond peeing on several sticks to confirm her pregnancy, Rosie hadn't done anything to adapt to this change in her circumstances. Perhaps it had been a form of denial, or a way of staving off the reality of this while she came to terms with being pregnant. AKA giving herself the space, and grace, to accept what her future would look like.

So it wasn't really a surprise that Aristotle—upon learning this—turned into some kind of pregnancy control freak, booking her an immediate appointment with a top London obstetrician, which included a full suite of blood tests and an ultrasound.

She tried to ignore the fact that Aristotle was by her side as the obstetrician smeared goopy liquid on her stomach and ran the wand over it. Tried to ignore the fact that he was only a foot away, staring at the same screen she was.

'Would you like to know the gender of the baby?'

Rosie's heart clenched. *The baby.* Tears formed in her eyes as she stared at the grainy image—their child, recognisably a little person, bobbling around. She pressed her teeth into her lip to stop from crying, shaking her head a little.

'I—no.' She glanced up at Aristotle, and then wished she hadn't. His face was like thunder—a storm about to burst. As though this was the worst confirmation he could have expected. He clearly wasn't riding the same emotional waves she was.

So why propose?

Why forcibly shoehorn himself into her life, this pregnancy?

It hadn't even occurred to her that he'd want a part of this.

It wasn't as if they'd ever had a relationship, or been

friends. At most, they'd shared a few interesting conversations over the years, but Rosie's feelings had been completely one-sided. A long-held childish crush that had morphed into meaningless sex. Twice, now.

But how could it be meaningless, when it had also fundamentally changed the course of her life?

He would always be her first lover, and now, the father of her baby.

'You're sure?' the sonographer asked kindly, glancing from Rosie to Aristotle, then back to Rosie.

'I think I'd rather be surprised.'

'You haven't been surprised enough?' Aristotle drawled, and her heart twisted.

'Okay,' the sonographer glossed over the awkwardness. 'We're all done. I'll have a report sent to the obstetrician. Will you be giving birth here?'

She opened her mouth to answer, but Aristotle spoke first. 'No. We're leaving for Athens tonight.'

Rosie startled, her gaze jerking swiftly to his. *What?* The question burst through her, but she managed to contain it—just. While she was all geared up to shout at this arrogant, bossy man, she didn't fancy doing so with an audience.

So she gritted her teeth and said nothing, waiting until they were out in the daylight before spinning to confront him.

'What the hell, Aristotle?'

He still looked as though he'd seen a ghost in there, but she refused to feel pity for him. He'd strong-armed his way into this situation; it wasn't her fault if he was suddenly finding the idea of parenthood unnerving.

'It's not too late to back out, you know,' she muttered when he didn't respond.

'Isn't it?'

She flinched. 'You really are a callous bastard.'

He closed his eyes then, expelling a sharp breath. 'I wasn't prepared for that.'

'Whereas I was?'

'No.' He stared at her, then almost through her, his eyes probing her in a way she found utterly unnerving. It was as though he had the ability to strip her apart, piece by piece, and reveal the fundamental make-up of her body. She shivered involuntarily.

'When did you find out?'

Summer was almost over and a hint of autumn breeze brushed past them, lifting Rosie's hair across her face, and Aristotle's gaze seemed to chase it, almost hungrily—so intensely that she felt as though he was touching her. She took an involuntary step backwards, warding off that feeling—and the temptation to do something stupid, like lean forward, closing the space between them.

'About a month ago,' she murmured. 'I had to get a blood test, for work. It's routine. The pregnancy was picked up on the screening.'

'You had no idea?'

She shook her head.

'So you didn't experience any symptoms?'

She shook her head again. 'I mean, looking back, my cycle had been different, but then, it's always been erratic, so I didn't notice much of a change. I've been a little tired, had a few headaches. I suppose I've been off some foods I would usually eat, but nothing that made me stop and go, "Uh-huh, I'm having a baby!"'

His features showed contemplation. 'Were you going to tell me?'

She opened her mouth to deny that, then clamped it shut again. What had seemed like an easy decision in the moment now sat like a bit of uneven ground between them, tricky to navigate. Given his reaction, and staunch insistence on being a huge part of their baby's life, her instincts about him had clearly been way off the mark.

'It's a yes or no question.'

'No.' Why lie? 'You'd made it clear how you felt.'

'About a hypothetical baby, but once you were pregnant, didn't it occur to you that it was different?'

'Honestly, I thought I was doing you a favour.'

His stubbled jaw shifted as though he was grinding his teeth.

'Come on, Aristotle. Nothing about you screams "paternal".'

His brows raised. 'Should I have a T-shirt made?'

It was the very last thing she'd expected him to say, and it had the strangest effect of lifting one side of her lips in an involuntary smile. She stifled it quickly, glancing away and lifting her hand to tuck her errant hair behind one ear. When she looked back at him, his eyes were busy boring into hers again.

'How do you feel?'

She frowned. 'In the sense of—'

'Pregnancy. Tired? Hungry?'

Both, but she wasn't about to admit either of those things to him. She couldn't say why, but it felt vital not to show a hint of weakness to this man.

Nor to ever, ever forget what he'd done to her, four years earlier. She'd lost her virginity to a guy who'd been dared to sleep with her. Her stomach rolled at the memory of that, at the pain she'd felt. It had lanced through her. How could she marry him? How could she raise a child with him, knowing what he was capable of?

'I'm fine.' Her voice was clipped.

'Then we have a few more stops to make.'

He continued to look at her, though, as if expecting her to argue.

She didn't. Whether pride, dignity or Stockholm syndrome, she fell into step beside him, to walk the short distance to his limousine. The driver was there, waiting, but it was Aristotle who reached for the rear passenger door and held it open for her.

As she stepped into the car she accidentally brushed against his arm, and her whole body exploded with a cacophony of recognition. She groaned inwardly at that physical betrayal. She hated this man—when was her damned libido going to get the message?

After the doctor's, his car had driven them to an exclusive Chelsea jeweller's. The store had been closed for Aristotle, so he and Rosie were left alone to browse. She had no interest in an engagement ring—or an engagement, for that matter—so left it to Aristotle to choose something.

Then wished she hadn't, when he selected a large solitaire diamond in a platinum four-claw setting. As he swiped a black credit card to pay for the thing, she couldn't help but smile to imagine herself turning up to an archaeological dig wearing something like this. Her colleagues would think she'd lost the plot. Or won the lottery.

The latter certainly wasn't true, but the former?

Was this madness?

Acquiescing to him, taking him at his word that he'd fight her tooth and nail to get full custody of this baby? She'd been bowled over by his arrival; she hadn't been given the space to think anything through. But now she looked at it objectively, it was almost impossible to believe that Aristotle would pick a fight with her, of all people.

While they might not like each other, his mother adored

her. Surely Melina would be able to talk her son down, to help him see that this wasn't the right plan of attack?

But what if she wasn't?

It was a gamble.

For all that Melina was his mother, they weren't close—something she'd heard Melina bemoan often enough. Aristotle respected his mother, and of course he must have loved her, too, but Rosie had no reason to think that Melina would be able to influence his actions. Or that anyone could, for that matter.

He'd always been like this.

She'd watched from afar. Not just in person but online as well, and she'd read enough articles in the papers to know that when Aristotle Machairas set his mind on something, heaven help anyone who tried to stand in his way.

'Do you need help packing?'

She hadn't even realised they'd reached her home.

She stared at him, frowning, the finality of this only hitting her then. The reality wrapping around her like a boa constrictor.

'There has to be another way,' she said, staring at his face, expression unknowingly haunted. Her hand pressed to her stomach, feeling the gentle roundness—their baby.

'Such as?'

Hope flared inside of her. 'Living in the same city. Seeing each other often.'

Memories of her parents' fights flooded her brain; that awful, post-traumatic response caused her skin to break out in blotchy pink. Her father had suggested that; Rosie was almost sure of it. But Moira had been adamant. Rosie was *hers*, and *hers alone*. If he wanted a divorce, then he'd lose Rosie, too.

She'd been a pawn for her mother, used to try to get her

father to stay, and then to punish him for leaving. Never mind that she'd been so close to him, so adored by him; Rosie had been too young to have any say in the outcome of their divorce.

Emotions thickened the walls of her throat so she found it hard to swallow, and tears stung her eyes. She blinked them away quickly.

'You really hate this, don't you?' he asked, staring at her without moving.

She nodded slowly.

His lips compressed into a gash on his face. 'There's no other way.'

'But we could—'

'No.' His voice was harsh, ringing with finality. 'I will not be sidelined from my child's life.'

She spun her engagement ring around her finger, the weight of the diamond something she wasn't used to.

'You don't need to marry me to be a part of their life. I'm not a monster, Aristotle. I have no interest in keeping you away from your baby, if you want to see them.'

'See them?' he repeated, tone incredulous. 'I've told you; I'm raising this child as mine. I have every intention of being as much a part of their life as you.' His gaze narrowed. 'Our baby will know they have two parents who love them enough to get married.'

She closed her eyes on a wave of frustration. 'What if that destroys them? Haven't you thought of that? We can't make each other happy—that's not ideal.'

'This isn't about our happiness.'

'That's not what I'm saying.' She sucked in a steadying breath, and tried again. 'My parents were miserable together. Not at first, I suppose, but by the time I was old enough to understand, I realised they were different to my friends' parents. They fought, pretty much around the clock. My dad gave me a set of headphones, and I would wear them all the time.' She twisted the ring faster. 'It's far better for two parents to raise a child separately than to try to make a marriage work when they hate one another.'

'I don't hate you,' he responded quietly, carefully. 'And I don't think you hate me, either.'

Her eyes flashed to his, memories of that night slicing through her anew. *'I can't believe you actually screwed her, man... We were just joking around... She's practically the hired help...'*

'You're wrong.' It felt so important to defend her twenty-year-old self in this way. To make him understand that her hatred was real, and soul-deep. 'You are everything I despise.'

His features didn't shift, so on some level, she wondered if he'd been expecting that. Almost looking for it.

'Then I presume your experience with your parents will inspire you to hide it from our child.'

His words landed against her heart with a dull thud. Of course, he was right. No matter the situation, she would move heaven and earth to avoid letting her child know the pain she'd lived with.

She blinked her tears away, focusing her attention on the street beyond the tinted windows of his limousine.

'What was your home like?'

She frowned, not understanding.

'When you were growing up. Where did you live?'

'Oh.' She cleared her throat. 'We had a place in Hammersmith.'

'Big? Small?'

'Two bedrooms. Why?'

'Because your parents couldn't escape one another. Whatever issues they had, they festered and built, until they argued.'

She didn't turn to face him; she didn't want him to see the surprise on her features. Because he was right. He'd so perfectly described the cloying, claustrophobic tension she'd grown up with.

'This won't be a problem for us.'

'Because your house is so big?'

'It's more than large enough to avoid one another, if needed.'

'You don't think you can annoy me from a distance?'

His lip quirked in something that might have been a smile. His eyes shifted beyond her, to the window, reminding Rosie that she was supposed to be going inside to pack a bag.

But before she could reach for the handle, he said, 'What did you listen to, Rosemary?'

She frowned. 'Huh?'

'When you were little, and they argued. You said he gave you headphones.'

'Oh.' She glanced to his face, wondering if he'd think her strange, then deciding she didn't care. 'The *Odyssey*.'

His brow arched with surprise. 'Homer?'

She nodded once. 'I always loved it. The heroism, the adventure.'

'And so the seeds were planted for your archaeological career.'

'Actually, I think that had more to do with those encyclopaedias of your mother's,' she said with a half-smile, missing the way thunderclouds briefly crossed his features. 'They introduced me to so many ancient wonders, sites that I itched to explore, even then. It was like the cracking open of a door I hadn't fully realised actually existed.'

But something had shifted between them. He nodded towards the apartment, then glanced at her. ‘Be quick; the plane is waiting.’

CHAPTER FOUR

APART FROM THE plane being insanely luxurious from tip to toe and every sumptuous detail in between, she couldn't help but notice the branding was different. Apart from the Machairas family logo she was familiar with, this boasted something else—a string of words in Greek.

There was no question the plane was his though. From the way he swaggered on board as though he, well, owned the place, to the clear deference of his staff, to the black leather upholstery with gold accents, this aircraft was Aristotle through and through.

And suddenly Rosie felt every bit the gauche young woman she'd always been around him. As a teenager, then at twenty. She glanced down at the simple shirt and skirt she'd pulled on that morning—what felt like a lifetime ago—and half wished she could avoid sitting down at all.

She hardly belonged on a plane like this.

God, what was she getting herself into?

This wasn't her.

She wasn't some billionaire's wife. Or the mother of his child, for that matter.

She was a free spirit, a woman with no ties other than to history, her major obligation to the fidelity of interpreting the past. Her job was to find its secrets, lovingly translate them and share, as she could, with the present.

To educate and inspire.

This was something else.

'You need to eat something.'

She blinked across at him as the engines roared to life.

'And you need to sit down.'

She just stood there, looking from Aristotle to the door, perhaps, in the back of her sluggish mind, wondering if it was too late to back out of this. To walk off the plane and never look back.

'*Christós*,' he muttered. 'Don't even think about it.'

And then, to her shock, and chagrin, two strong, broad hands were curving around her upper arms, drawing her towards one of the sleek leather armchairs. His touch was practical, but that didn't matter. It didn't stop the flames that curled and licked across her skin, the goosebumps that trembled across her. It didn't stop her from breathing in and catching a hint of his masculine fragrance and remembering what it had been like, that afternoon in the courtyard of his mother's villa, when Aristotle had driven into her as though the passions of all time were at his back.

She was a student of history, and the one thing that always resonated with her was the familiarity of the basic human condition. Certain traits and emotions that were embodied by people across time. It was a uniquely bonding experience to look upon the ruins of Pompeii and see people clutching at each other in their final moments. Realising that at the end of all time, their sole comfort came from companionship.

Passion was another such emotion, in all its destructive urgency. What better way was there to define what had taken place between them? Like the bringing together of an accelerant and spark, after four years, they'd been together barely five minutes and it had ignited.

'Sit,' he commanded, needlessly, because his hands had welded her to the chair. Or perhaps it was that his touch had weakened her knees sufficiently for him to be able to fold her downwards without any opposition.

The plane began to push back. Unlike on a commercial jet, there was no safety video, no flight attendant walking the aisle to check that they were properly *in situ*. Everything was left to them. Well, to Aristotle. Rosie had turned into an incompetent gaping fish.

With an exhalation of impatience, his hands were at her hips then, reaching for the discreet seatbelt, bringing it across her lap and fastening it.

She jumped, hurtling back into the present, shoving her gaping fish persona behind a wall of irritation. 'I can do it, for goodness' sake!'

His eyes flicked to hers, his expression sheer mockery. 'Can you? Show me.'

With a mutinous expression, she moved to take the seatbelt, but his hands were there, and it was impossible not to brush against them. Those same fires licked and flamed across her flesh. Before she could stop it, a breath hissed from between her teeth.

Now his expression displayed something other than mockery. Something far more dangerous, because it reflected the heat that was stirring in her veins. A shiver ran the length of her spine as memories flooded her before she could control them. His touch, his mouth, his whole self.

'Aristotle—' She said his name on a soft exhalation that came dangerously close to a plea. She blinked quickly, pulling back, clinging to whatever threads of sanity she could find.

He seemed to do the same, straightening, hands falling to his sides before he turned and moved to the chair opposite. She couldn't help but notice how much of the seat he took up with his large, broad frame, his arms resting on the sides.

She swallowed quickly, tamping down on the last embers of need.

'We should talk about the wedding.'

The plane began to move faster down the runway, the perfect metaphor for the juggernaut she'd climbed aboard. The way he said that so matter-of-factly—'the wedding'—as though there was no doubt in his mind that this was happening.

Her eyes dropped to the enormous ring, the visual confirmation that she had, in fact, agreed to this.

'What about it?'

'It makes sense to marry as soon as we can arrange it.'

Her throat seemed to be tightening unbearably.

'In terms of the ceremony itself, I presume you have some thoughts on what you'd like?'

She stared at him, drawing a complete blank. 'No, actually. I've never thought about it.'

'Getting married?'

She shook her head. 'Nope.'

'Why not?'

She pulled a face. 'Is that relevant?'

'Given that we're about to get married, yes.'

Fair point.

'I just never really planned on doing the whole wedding thing,' she said, lifting one shoulder, as the plane began to climb into the sky, gaining altitude quickly.

'Interesting.'

'Is it?'

'You always struck me as someone who believed in romantic fairytales.'

She rolled her eyes. 'Because I'm a woman?'

'Because you were forever reading, most of the time, romances.'

She ignored the strange lurching in her stomach that came from his unspoken admission that he'd *seen* her, as a teenager. Back when she'd presumed herself invisible to the tall, older, beautiful guy she'd been swooning over from afar.

Heat flooded her cheeks and she blinked towards the windows, taking a second to steady her breath.

'Reading romance doesn't mean you believe in it.'

'You're saying you don't?'

'After what happened with you? How could I.'

The words were out before she could stop them, and she felt heat spread to the roots of her hair. She hadn't meant to say that. To admit to him how much his behaviour had affected her. Besides, her aversion to 'happily ever after' went way back, to a time before she even knew the name Aristotle Machairas.

His frown was reflexive, his eye's holding hers for a beat too long, in a way that made her insides lurch.

'I didn't know you were a virgin.'

She shook her head, not wanting to talk about it.

'You made that clear. Anyway, I was joking. I mean, the experience with you was hardly the best, but you're really only partly to blame. My belief in happy endings was destroyed a long time before I met you.'

His lips compressed and she held her breath, wondering if he was going to let what had happened between them go, or push her further on it.

'Because of your parents,' he said eventually.

A noise behind her heralded the arrival of a flight attendant, carrying a tray with water and snacks.

It wasn't until that moment she realised how hungry she was.

The flight attendant slid a table out from the wall, clicked it into place, then set the food and drinks down between them. Rosie was glad for the distraction. This conversation was somehow too close to the truth for comfort.

'How old were you when they divorced?' he asked casually.

So, they weren't moving on then, after all.

She sighed. 'Nine.'

He frowned. 'And they fought most of your childhood?'

'I don't remember a time where they weren't fighting,' she admitted.

'So why not divorce sooner?'

'It was just a toxic environment,' she murmured, reaching for the water and taking a sip.

'How so?'

She pulled a face. 'Does this matter?'

'For various reasons, yes.'

'What reasons?'

'We're about to have a child together, so understanding you and your values seems important. Secondly, your father is married to my mother. If the environment was so toxic, it would be nice to know history isn't repeating itself.'

She stared at him with a strange sense of betrayal forming inside of her. 'Are you using me to get to my dad?'

A muscle jerked in his jaw. 'My father died less than a year before their wedding.'

'I know how hard that must have been for you,' she said gently.

His nostrils flared.

'They became friends, over the years. Your father, mother, my father. They treated him like an equal. After your father's death, I know your mother turned to Dad for comfort, familiarity. Their relationship caught them both by surprise.'

A muscle pulsed in his jaw. 'Prior to marrying my mother—who is worth tens of billions of dollars in her own right—and becoming "friends" with my parents, your father was her chauffeur. You don't think I have a right to be a little concerned?'

'They've been married—happily, I might add—for years. Not that you'd know, you're never even around. So don't sit there and act all protective and invested in your mother's life, Aristotle. I don't buy it.'

His eyes were impossible to read, but there was a darkness swirling in their depths that might have made someone else panic. Not Rosie. She'd already run the gamut of emotions with this man; he couldn't scare her, no matter how darkly brooding his expression.

She reached for the glass and took another sip of water. When she settled back in her seat, it was to find his gaze still on her face.

'You're saying the fights were your mother's fault?'

She opened her mouth to respond then clamped it shut, taking a moment to process that.

'Relationships are complicated,' she said thoughtfully. 'I think my mother was very hurt by Dad's leaving, and that she made some terrible decisions.' She blinked away from him, wishing she could so easily blot out the painful memories of that time in her life. 'She used me to hurt him, because she loved him so much,' she said quietly, surprised that the words almost seemed to rush out of her, as though desperate to be shared. A pain she hated to contemplate, and a deeply held insecurity that if she let herself love she might turn into her mother gripped her heart, making it hard to speak for a moment. 'Six months went by, in which she refused to let me see him.'

'How is that possible?'

Rosie hesitated, even now feeling a loyalty to her mother, despite everything that had happened.

'She said he was abusive.'

Aristotle was so silent, she turned to look at him, to see if he'd heard. It was clear from the tightening in his jaw that he had, but she couldn't fathom what he was thinking.

'I presume he wasn't?' His voice was held perfectly level.

'Never,' she disputed. 'You might not like how quickly they got married after your dad passed away, but you *know* my father. You must know he's one of the kindest, most gentle souls that's ever lived.'

Aristotle's eyes narrowed slightly.

'Not to mention, he's got top level police clearance. He had to, for the positions he's held.'

Aristotle tilted his head once.

'She almost jeopardized everything for him—his work, his relationship with me.' She shook her head with a hint of anger. She'd long ago come to terms with the desperation her mother had felt, that had driven her to such a low act. 'She wasn't in a good place,' Rosie explained. 'It was basically a huge disaster.'

'And yet she retained custody of you.'

She nodded. 'Even after everything that had happened, Dad thought it was for the best, for both of us. That Mum needed me.'

'And what would have been best for you?'

She blinked quickly. How had she revealed so much to him? She'd never spoken so freely about this to anyone, even her father. These were wounds she kept buried deep, deep inside.

'My mother did need me,' she admitted. 'At first, anyway. After a couple of years, she met someone else, got married, had other children. I was sent to boarding school.'

'Why not to live with your father?'

She dropped her gaze. 'She still didn't want him to have me.'

He leaned forward in his chair on a soft curse, and his frame was large enough that with that one simple act he brought himself close enough to make it hard for her to breathe. They weren't touching, and yet it felt almost as though he was invading every single one of her senses.

'Hearing you talk about your childhood makes me think you understand this,' he said, voice deep and raw. 'We can give our child so much more than you had.'

'But what if we can't?' she whispered. 'What if we fight, like they fought?'

His eyes were locked to hers in a way she found it impossible to look away from. 'We won't.'

And he spoke with such confidence that she found it impossible to doubt him.

'We will also have an iron-clad prenuptial agreement that will include custodial arrangements, should it ever reach the point we cannot make this marriage a success.'

She frowned. 'Then why can't we just fast forward to that?'

'Because I would prefer to raise the baby together.'

She shook her head. 'That makes no sense.'

'We try the marriage,' he said, voice firm. 'If it really doesn't work, we have options, but I am not prepared to give up before we've started.'

Strangely, she'd gone from viewing this marriage with panic, to pragmatism. He was right, on so many levels. It made a very weird sort of sense, to marry him for the sake of their baby, and the life they could give it. Her child would never know the pain of feeling torn between warring parents. She didn't like Aristotle—at all—but that didn't mean they couldn't form a truce, of sorts, in the interest of the baby.

'So, the wedding,' he said, staying where he was, and returning the conversation to the original topic. 'Would you like to invite many friends? Shall we book a large venue? I can have my jet bring anyone over from the UK that you'd like included.'

'Friends,' she repeated, stricken. Not because thoughts of her own friends and colleagues left her cold, but because thoughts of his *did*. If she had her friends at the wedding, wouldn't he have his?

'Are you…inviting many people?'

His expression shifted slightly. 'I don't see the point,' he said after a beat, shrugging one shoulder. 'Our wedding matters most to us, and our families. But if you'd like to turn it into a bigger affair, I won't stand in your way.'

'No,' she blurted out quickly. She couldn't bear the thought of coming face to face with his friends again. Not after the conversation she'd overheard four and a half years earlier.

'At least she's got nice breasts... And you're a hundred thou richer, not that you need it...'

So degrading. So awfully judgemental and rude. Even now, her cheeks heated with shame and hurt, anger and impotence.

She wished she'd stayed and confronted them all. Mostly, she wished she'd confronted Aristotle—told him she'd heard, that she knew he'd slept with her on a dare. Such a cruel, callous thing to have done.

She wished she'd stayed and listened to the rest, instead of turning on her heel and running away, biting back a sob until she was sure no one would hear. Yet even now, embarrassment and mortification held her tongue still, so she didn't say any of the things she'd thought over the years. The fitting insults she'd wished she'd hurled at his feet.

It was like being doused in ice water. She felt it trickle through her veins, filling her with dread.

How could she be marrying this man? Having his baby?

'Fine. Small and intimate. Would the chapel at my mother's house suit?'

The chapel was one of the oldest buildings on the Machairas land. Old stone that had been rendered a creamy white, with a red terracotta roof and arched windows down either side, it was at a high point of the sprawling estate, with sweeping views out over the city. She could still vividly remember the first time she'd discovered it, as a teenager. She'd pushed open the heavy timber door, not really expecting it to give, and sucked in a deep breath when it had. Like magic, she'd thought at the time. The building had smelled musty, but that hadn't mattered. She'd crept over the wide timber floorboards, running her hands across the pews as she travelled up the aisle. From the windows at the front, a huge bougainvillea could be seen, with splashes of almost neon pink a dramatic contrast to the cerulean blue of the sky. She'd stood there and held her breath, wondering if there was any place more perfect on earth.

She still couldn't say she'd found one.

'That will be fine,' she responded, ignoring the twisting in her heart. She'd come to understand the history of the chapel, on successive visits to Greece. Long before Melina was her stepmother, she'd taken Rosie under her wing, perhaps sensing, even then, a fellow lover of times long gone.

She'd talked about each of the buildings on the estate, their provenance, their significance. Rosie knew, therefore, that for generations the Machairas family's lives had been celebrated in this chapel—funerals, baptisms, and yes, weddings.

Though her father and stepmother had married instead from a large room in the house, and Rosie had understood that. The death of Kyrios Machairas had been so recent. As Aristotle had said, less than a year before their wedding, his funeral had been held in the chapel.

'Now, let's talk about how we tell them.' Aristotle's tone was businesslike once more, drawing her attention back to the present.

'Tell who what?'

'Your father and my mother.'

Her stomach dropped to the very bottom of the earth. She stared at him, lips parting.

Of *course* they had to be told, but Rosie hadn't imagined the actual act of breaking this news. She twisted her fingers, imagining her dad's kindly face when he learned this. He'd probably be relieved to discover that her determination to never marry and have children had been set aside. Not to mention the fact it prevented her from travelling to some of the dangerous dig sites she tended to opt for.

'Given the timeline,' he said, nodding towards her stomach, 'sooner makes sense.'

'Yes, of course.' She blew a breath from between her lips, steadying herself for what was to come. 'You think it's better if we pretend this is legitimate?'

He arched a brow. 'Us?'

She nodded.

'I imagine we'll face less opposition if we claim to be romantically involved,' he said. 'But I'm happy to go with your preference.'

She considered that. They could be honest, and tell them they were marrying to give the baby a stable home, so that they could both be fully in their child's life. On some level, they might respect that.

Except her father wouldn't.

He would have all the same objections Rosie had felt.

Marrying someone you couldn't stand had the potential to be a disaster. He wouldn't want that for Rosie. He'd never accept their wedding, and she couldn't bear the thought of upsetting him.

'You're right,' she said, her insides rolling at what they were agreeing to. 'It's going to be easier if we just pretend to be a couple around them.'

She flicked a glance to him, unknowing dread across her features.

'You hate the thought of that,' he murmured.

'I'm not a good liar.'

'Says the woman who was preparing to conceal a child's parentage from her closest family.'

Heat flooded her cheeks.

'A necessity.' As was the little white lie she'd told her father about having a boyfriend, the night of Melina's party. She'd wanted to avoid any possible risk of their parents finding out about what they'd done. It seemed like a moot point now.

'As it turned out, it's not.'

'Yeah, well…' Her voice tapered off as she realised they were getting drawn off course. 'So, we'll pretend, around them.'

'And we will see them together as rarely as possible,' he said.

She nodded. 'That works.'

'Fine. Would you prefer me to visit them alone first? To explain, and ask your father's permission?'

She stared at him as though he'd suggested she start wearing shoes on her hands. 'What?'

'He seems traditional.'

She blanched. 'No.' Her dispute was swift. 'For a start, you're the last man on earth who would plausibly ask anyone for permission to do *anything*. To say nothing of the fact I hate the whole concept of asking for permission to marry me. I'm not some piece of property that can be traded from him to you.' She shuddered. 'Secondly, we should tell them together. We'll go there, act happy and...'

'In love,' he prompted, eyes showing mockery.

'Or whatever.' She waved a hand in the air, mentally disparaging the concept of being in love—and particularly with this man. 'Honestly, if you were to ask, I doubt he'd give you the answer you wanted, anyway.'

'He doesn't like me.'

'He wouldn't think you're good enough for me,' she said. 'Then again, he probably wouldn't think anyone was.'

'I see. Because you're such a catch?'

She refused to register the pain spiralling through her. Memories of his rejection, his friends' cruel taunts, the way he'd stood there and listened to them without saying anything in her defence. She angled her face away, ignoring the hurt that was spreading over her like a wave.

'We'll tell them together,' she said firmly. 'We'll do it quickly, then we'll leave, and go back to pretending one another doesn't exist.'

He didn't respond, which she took to be his way of agreeing.

He had never known anyone who could drive him into a fit of fury as quickly as Rosemary Richardson. She sparred with him in a way no one else would *dare*, and far from taking the high road and letting her spit and fume and get things off her chest, he flung himself right down into the mud-pit with her.

'Because you're such a catch?'

He'd been angry at her summation of Glen Richardson's likely response to this 'engagement'. Angry because, without knowing it, she'd pressed her fingers on a pain point he'd carried for a long time—a pain point he hated because it made him vulnerable and weak.

That he wasn't good enough. That he wasn't worth anything.

It didn't matter how much he succeeded in life, the vulnerable teenager who'd learned the truth of his adoption and had his whole world shaken to its core was still a part of him, and when Rosemary hurled those insults at his feet she stirred that teenager back to life.

The truth was, objectively, Rosemary was, in fact, a catch. Beautiful, intelligent, interesting, well-read and well-travelled, the fact she wasn't in a relationship was a testament to how her upbringing had affected her, rather than there being anything fundamentally undesirable about her.

The opposite was true.

He'd spent the entire flight working overtime to pretend he wasn't noticing the way she gently flicked the ends of her hair, or toyed with her fingers, or crossed and uncrossed her legs, so he wanted to reach out and put his hand on her knee, curving it over her, holding her still. Telling her it was going to be okay, even when he wasn't sure that was true.

Because this whole thing was an unmitigated disaster, something he had spent his adult life assiduously avoiding: marriage, and children. Yet here he was, flying towards a future he would have said he didn't want, with a woman he couldn't stand.

And there was nothing either of them could do about it.

CHAPTER FIVE

'WAIT.' SHE PACED the gravel driveway, fingers pressed to her lips. 'I can't do this.'

Aristotle stood his ground, arms crossed over his chest. 'Which part?'

'This.' She twisted her engagement ring. 'All of it. The engagement. Marrying you. Telling them.' She looked anxiously towards the mansion. 'Aristotle, this is a mistake.'

His lips pursed. 'You're pregnant with my baby. There is no alternative.'

'But surely we can—'

'I misspoke. There is one alternative,' he said, lifting a finger into the air, holding it between them.

She stopped walking and stared at him, her stomach in loops. 'Court.'

He dipped his head once. 'I have lawyers currently preparing our wedding documents, but if you'd prefer, I can brief them instead for a custody hearing.'

She felt the blood drain from her face. 'Aristotle,' she whispered, tears springing to her eyes, surprising her. She blamed pregnancy hormones. She was under no illusions when it came to this man's awful, hateful ways.

For the briefest moment, something shifted in his expression. Regret? Sympathy? Something soft. But then, his features tightened into a mask of determination.

'I will not have my child doubt my commitment to them.'

Her brow furrowed at the intensity of his statement. The feeling behind the words.

'Why would they? We can make sure that doesn't happen.'

A muscle throbbed at the base of his stubbled jaw, drawing her gaze there, to the pulse.

She wasn't able to reply though. Before she could form a cogent argument, much less put it into words, the front door pushed open and Melina Machairas flew out, her elegant figure—tall and slim ever since Rosie had met her—dressed in an expensive-looking trouser suit, her long salt-and-pepper hair pulled into a neat plait.

'Oh, Rosie, you're home. Thank you, my darling, you did it,' she said, moving first to Aristotle and embracing him, as Rosie's father stood in the doorframe to the house, observing the scene. It all happened so fast, and yet to Rosie it was almost as though time stood still. She was conscious of every detail of the scene, from the moment Melina wrapped her in a huge hug, smelling of roses and vanilla, then reached down and took hold of Rosie's hand—her fingers brushing over the ring a moment before surprise and realisation crossed her face.

'Rosie? What is this?' She held Rosie's hand up, studying the ring, looking from Rosie to Glen with a broadening smile. 'Darling, who's the lucky man?'

Her mind went blank. Completely and utterly, uselessly blank. She gaped at her stepmother, then over her shoulder to Aristotle. He was looking at Rosie with an inscrutable expression. Saying nothing, leaving it up to her.

Marriage, or custody dispute. Which he would undoubtedly win.

But there was more to consider, like his assertion that this child would be better with both of them in their lives. If they could make this work, wasn't that likely? There were so many advantages to this marriage, including her ability, when she was ready, to travel for work, and know that her child would be safely cared for. She'd never leave for long, of course, but at least she'd have the option to do some consulting trips.

It was the passion in his voice though, when he'd said, *'I will not have my child doubt my commitment to them',* that strangely served to convince her of the rightness of this. It was making the best of a bad situation.

'Actually, that's what we came to talk to you about,' she said, after a beat. Now, when she glanced at Aristotle, she saw triumph in his eyes. She tamped down on an answering emotion. Frustration, yes, but also, damn it, desire. Because this version of him—take charge, know-it-all, arrogant executive—was tantalizingly powerful and sexier than sin. And how she hated him for that.

'That would be me,' he said, taking a step towards Rosie and shocking her then by sliding a hand possessively around her waist, drawing her to his side.

She wasn't used to this new role she'd been thrust into and shock must have shown on her features when she jerked her face towards his, because his eyes narrowed with unspoken warning and then, as if to ram home what he'd just said—to all of them—he dropped his head and kissed her, then and there.

Even as he kissed her, he knew it was a mistake. A mistake to do this now, here, in front of his mother, her father.

A mistake to kiss her, knowing that his baby was growing inside of her, sparking all sorts of caveman ideologies he'd never knowingly ascribed to.

He'd kissed her twice before, and each time had become a fire that raged out of control, culminating in sex. Hot, fast sex. And though neither of them was going to strip naked here and now, the same undeniable spark of passion flared to life as though they were completely alone.

The kiss had been borne of necessity—designed to convince the witnesses of something they might otherwise doubt. And also to remind Rosemary of the parts they were to play. But the second his lips pressed to hers, demanding and insistent, her whole body had gone soft against him, moulding to him perfectly, so his hands had itched to reacquaint themselves with her generous curves—including the changes.

He kissed her and in the back of her throat he heard the moaning with which he was intimately familiar, as her hand slid around to the small of his back and pressed there, fingers wide. Every part of him grew hard in anticipation. He pulled back moments before that choice was lost to him, staring down at her with a sense that he was in freefall.

Damn this woman.

'What the hell?'

Glen Richardson's voice went some of the way to cutting through the fog of need that had swamped them both. He took a small step away from Rosemary, but kept an arm around her back. For support or closeness, he couldn't say. His fingers, on her hip, moved rhythmically, small motions up and down, tempting him with the gentle curve there, making him itch to slip inside the waistband of her skirt and feel her bare flesh.

Both times they'd made love, she'd been wearing clothes.

The first time, he'd been completely caught off-guard by what had happened. Urgency had overcome him, and her shirt had been left in place, revealing only the outline of her full, rounded breasts to his hungry gaze. The second time had been so fast, her dress in place the entire time. It was a shame, not to have ever revelled in her nakedness and explored her body as a lover should—slow and thorough.

'Is this true, darling ones?' His mother's tone was noticeably happier.

'Yes.' He spoke swiftly, eyes lifting to Glen's face now and staying there. 'We're getting married.'

'But—why?' his mother asked.

Aristotle turned a droll expression on her. 'Isn't it obvious?'

A glance at Rosemary showed her cheeks were delightfully flushed. He reached over with his spare hand and brushed a finger over them, feeling the heat. She looked up at him, lips parted on a quick rush of breath.

'Now, wait, just a minute.' Glen reached them and stood toe to toe with Aristotle. But it was Rosemary he addressed. 'You don't need to do this.'

He felt her stiffen at his side and for a moment he was worried that she'd back out, rejecting him, reminding him that no one needed him and never would.

'I know that,' she said, though, softly, reaching out and wrapping her fingers over her dad's hand. 'I want to.'

'You want to marry Aristotle?' he said, looking from one to the other, as if it made no sense.

'Why are you surprised?' she pushed.

'Well, for one thing, you barely know each other. For another, you've got nothing in common.'

'We've known each other since I was fourteen,' she said.

Out of nowhere, that vision of Rosemary, the first time

they'd met, speared him. Her wide, curious eyes, her ready smile.

'You've met, yes, but that's not the same as knowing each other.'

'We didn't want to say anything,' Rosemary was continuing, and in the back of his mind, he had to admit he was impressed with how she was rolling with this, improvising calmly enough to convince the most astute audience. 'Until we were sure it was serious. Because of you guys.' She gestured from one to the other. 'There was no sense getting anyone's hopes up, until we knew it was worth mentioning.'

Melina moved into their field of vision, her smile making it obvious how she felt. She put her hands on Rosemary's forearms, tears in her eyes. 'I could not be happier,' she said. 'I have loved you like a daughter for as long as I've known you. The fact you will now be both my stepdaughter and daughter-in-law is a dream come true.' Then she reached out, pressing a hand to Rosemary's stomach. 'Not to mention, I'll be the grandmother of your baby.'

Aristotle clenched his jaw. He bit back the rejoinder that, strictly speaking, she wasn't. No more than she was his mother. Somewhere out there, another woman held that role—not that she'd cared enough to claim it.

'How long has this been going on?' Glen asked, looking considerably less pleased. Aristotle's hand resumed its tracking over Rosemary's hip, so he felt the moment she shivered and brought her closer to his side, folding her against his hard planes, relishing the softness of her curves.

'It's been a while,' Rosemary said noncommittally. 'But it was at your birthday—' she addressed Melina '—that we realised we were in love.'

The word slammed into him like a grenade, landing in

his throat and threatening to detonate, making it impossible to contemplate speaking.

Love.

He instantly dismissed the word and the concept.

No matter what else she was, Rosemary was a first-rate actress, though. He almost felt convinced by her schmaltzy performance.

'Well, well, this is most certainly a time for champagne!' Melina said, clasping her hands together. 'Non-alcoholic for you, of course.' She spun on her heel, smiling up at her husband then, who finally broke the sternness of his gaze to regard Melina.

'Yes, let's go inside,' he said gruffly, turning and stalking towards the door, Melina chatting happily at his side.

Rosie expelled a sharp breath, staying right where she was, pinned to Aristotle, even though their audience was almost in the house.

'You did well.' His voice was deep and gruff. She turned to face him…which was a mistake. They were so close that looking at him like this brought his lips back into focus, as well as memories of how it had been to be kissed by him again. For four months, the memory of what had happened in the courtyard on Melina's birthday weekend had been a nightly torture, a form of sensual drugging, because she'd been unable to escape the power of that recollection. To feel the aching, yearning memory of being held by him.

And for a moment, those feelings had come rushing back to her.

But this was a man who'd taken her virginity for a dare, she reminded herself. She owed the twenty-year-old version of herself more than this—more than standing like some clingy limpet at his side, looking up at him as though he was God's gift to women.

So why didn't she move, then? Why did she stay where she was, her body seeking the warmth of his, her hip almost happy-dancing at the feeling of his touch through the fabric of her shorts?

'They're looking,' he murmured, eyes flicking to the door. She glanced in their direction to see that yes, Glen and Melina had indeed stopped walking, and were standing arm in arm at the entrance of the house.

Her heart leapt to her throat as she turned back to Aristotle. This time, when her eyes landed on his mouth, she made no attempt to relocate their focus.

'I'm going to kiss you again,' he murmured, low, softly, so his lips barely moved.

She nodded slowly, one hand lifting to his shirt and catching the fabric between her fingers, scrunching it in her palm.

He dropped his head and brushed his lips over hers, slow and soft this time. As if he was reading her. But she didn't want that—softness had no place with them.

Her hand gripped his shirt harder and her lips parted against his, allowing his skilful tongue to sweep inside her mouth and duel with hers, to dominate her in that way he had. This time, his hand moved to her back and pushed her forward, so she felt the full force of his arousal through their clothes, pressed close to her sex, and she made a mewling noise deep in her throat as she lifted up onto the tips of her toes to give him better access to her mouth, to more ably convey the need that was flooding her.

Her hand moved from his bunched-up shirt to his shoulder, then curved behind his neck, finding the dark hair there and toying with it, before her other hand shifted to do the same thing. Her breasts were pressed against his chest, soft to hard, and with the hand that was shielded from view of Glen and Melina he cupped one breast, until she whimpered into his mouth. He broke the kiss then and dropped his hand, staring down at her with a look she could barely understand.

Surprise.

Shock.

Resentment.

It was enough to break the spell.

She quickly looked towards the door to see, with relief, that her father and stepmother had disappeared inside. They were alone, that completely private display of passion still private, thank God. She didn't particularly want anyone to witness the way he could so easily send her tipping over the edge.

How pathetic was she, after all that had come before, to turn into putty in his hands at the slightest touch?

'That shouldn't have happened,' she muttered, pulling away from him quickly, sucking in a deep breath and brushing her hands down her front, as though she could erase the effect of his touch so easily.

'And yet, when we're with them, it is inevitable.'

She closed her eyes. 'I think my dad could do without seeing that.'

A mocking smirk shaped his lips for a moment, before he sobered. 'Believe me, in the privacy of my home, I won't be making this mistake again.'

Mistake.

Her heart twisted, and she was that twenty-year-old girl again, with stars in her eyes for the man she'd believed Aristotle to be, getting her heart torn to shreds by the cruel jibes of his so-called friends.

Entitled, spoiled rich kids who saw someone like her as beneath them.

It was just the reminder she needed to stiffen her spine with steel. 'Let's get this over with, Aristotle. I'm finding it exhausting, having to pretend I don't hate you. The sooner we can get on with it, the better.'

She walked towards the house without waiting for a response.

Strangely, she'd never really thought of Aristotle's life outside of the estate. He was rarely home, at his mother's, and yet she never imagined *where* he lived. In her mind, when she thought of him, it was just *him*. Aristotle took up all of the space. Place was irrelevant.

However, if she'd given it any runtime whatsoever, she might have imagined him somewhere like this. In the penthouse of a ritzy modern building in the famously exclusive suburb of Kolonaki, high on Lycabettus Hill, with sweeping views of the city.

While she couldn't fault the outlook, the penthouse itself was both austere and intimidating. Oh, beautiful, of course, in that sterile, modernistic sort of way, like some kind of livable art installation, from the floor-to-ceiling windows to the expansive white marble-tiled floor, to the light fittings that were more like sculptures. It was all so cold and impersonal, so unlived-in, despite the fact it was where he presumably spent most of his time.

Just getting into his apartment had required a security protocol worthy of some kind of embassy, from the biometric scanning in the underground car park to the armed security guards who'd stood sentry at the elevator doors, to the finger-pad access he'd used to get inside.

'You don't approve?' he asked, shaking out of his suit jacket and draping it over the back of a chair. She watched the movement with a frown on her face, thinking that the mess seemed so wrong in here.

She looked around, frown deepening. 'Does it matter?'

'If it's to be your home, you should probably like it.'

'I didn't think this marriage is about what I want at all.'

'Don't do that,' he said, coming to stand in front of her, a big wall of muscly chest and temptation.

'What?' Irritation made her voice tremble. She couldn't help it. She was tired and sore in the lower back, and the situation with her father and stepmother had been more emotionally draining than she'd anticipated.

Scratch that, the whole thing with Aristotle had been.

'Don't act like you've been bullied into this.'

'I beg your pardon, that's exactly what you've done.'

His eyes were awash with something—something real and raw that made her think he actually had *real* feelings locked deep inside his cold, controlling persona, but it was gone almost instantly.

'We are both making sacrifices for our child.'

She ground her teeth, pain flaring at his description of their marriage, even when she knew it to be accurate. That was what they were doing.

'We are making the best of a bad situation,' he corrected, unknowingly making everything worse.

Maternal instincts fired to life. 'Not one part of me thinks of this life as a "bad situation".'

'You know what I mean,' he responded. 'Do you want a tour?'

She looked around again, shivering involuntarily. How could a man with red-hot passion in his veins live in an ice palace like this? Though that view, she thought, her gaze sweeping across the cold tiled floor and staring out at the city, was magnificent. Dusk had fallen, turning the sky into candy floss hues of pink and orange, and the Acropolis was glowing golden.

'Rosemary?'

She glanced across at him. 'Why do you call me that?'

'It's your name.'

'But everyone calls me Rosie.'

His eyes narrowed. 'It doesn't suit you.'

Something pricked deep in her chest as his expression assumed a deep, contemplative look.

'You just seem like Rosemary to me.'

She pulled a face. 'Why?'

'Rosie is frivolous. Silly. You always struck me as someone intelligent. A thinker.'

Her stomach seemed to twist out of her body. She shook her head, dismissing what could only be described as a compliment. Her first ever from Aristotle?

'Would you prefer I call you Rosie?'

Hearing it on his lips, in his accent, had her body grating with rejection. He was the only person in her life who called her Rosemary and suddenly she liked that. She shook her head once, maintaining a terse expression on her features even when there was a strange warmth—completely at odds with the barren iciness of this space—spreading through her.

'I don't care,' she lied. 'And yes, a tour would be great. I might as well see which part of this mausoleum I'm to call home.'

CHAPTER SIX

HE'D NEVER NOTICED that there was a certain starkness to the penthouse until he saw it through Rosemary's eyes. He'd never thought about it. The place had ticked all his boxes, most importantly, the security aspect. The building was shared by other high-profile individuals who valued privacy, and the complex was like a fortress. His own apartment was big enough to offer everything he could ever need, but the facilities of the building were second to none—including a rooftop helipad. The view was also exceptional, reminding him in some ways of the view from his parents' estate. And yet this epitome of modernity was as far removed from the ancient, sprawling estate as one could get. And for that, he was eternally grateful.

It was his home away from home, except neither was really a 'home'. His parents' estate had ceased feeling like that from the moment he'd discovered his adoption and confronted his father. And this?

It was only seeing Rosemary's slightly dazed expression as her wide green eyes swept across the details of each room that made him realise that. He had added only a few personal effects since moving in. His clothes, a state-of-the-art office and gym, and that was pretty much it.

'It's very…grey,' she said pensively, flicking a glance at

him and frowning in a way that almost made him laugh. She looked at him as though he had morphed into some kind of inhuman monster—though hadn't he always been that to her?

No. Not always. As a teenager, she'd been helpless to hide the way she looked at him. He couldn't be back in Greece without finding her staring at him, watching him, her cheeks flushing pink if he glanced in her direction. He remembered the way his friends had called him out on it, at his twenty-first birthday. He hadn't wanted a party, but his parents had insisted. Rosemary had happened to be there—it coincided with her school holidays—and from that point on, she'd become the butt of the joke to his one-time friends.

His gut twisted when he remembered some of the things they'd said about her—that he'd let them say because he'd been so angry with her, for the way she'd swept into his parents' home and seemingly taken his place. For the way his mother loved her, which made him despise her. It wasn't until the night of his mother's wedding that Aristotle had finally had enough of their cruel, insensitive, demeaning comments and told them all to take a damn hike. Not because of Rosemary, but because they'd crossed into generalized misogyny, and he didn't hold any quarter with that kind of talk. Treating women like meat, as though sex with them could be turned into some kind of game… It had sickened and disgusted him.

'I mean, it's fine,' she quickly added, frowning, looking back to the room he'd just presented as hers.

She stepped into the space, moving disastrously close to the bed. Reminding him that for all they'd slept together twice, neither of those occasions had been in a bed. And yet there was one just a few feet away from her, all made up, big and soft and…

'I think I'll need to paint it,' she said apologetically, nose scrunching up a little. As though she was afraid he might say no.

'Rosemary, you can paint anything. You can buy whatever furniture suits, change the artwork. This is now your home—act like it.'

Her eyes widened as though the reality of that was just sinking in. She looked around again, but this time it was with a spark of intent.

'Okay.' She nodded, moving towards the curtains and pulling them open, her gaze falling on the spectacular view. 'It's so lovely.' She sighed to emphasise that. 'It's funny, for all I'm an archaeologist, I've done very little work in Greece.'

He tamped down on the part of him that was blaring with a clear warning sign. This whole situation would work better if they kept things on a businesslike footing. He didn't need to know the whole backstory to her life.

'Why is that?' he asked anyway, moving further into the room.

'Good question. On the one hand, most of these sites have been explored again and again.'

'So there's less chance of a new discovery?'

'Oh, there's always a chance,' she said, flicking her eyes towards him as her lips lifted in a small smile. 'I suppose I just like to follow the path less travelled.'

'Where have you worked?'

He told himself not to move towards her. To stay safely on the other side of the bedroom. It was a large space—at least twice the size of her apartment in Putney. She put her hand on her stomach, gaze returning to the sparkling view of Athens.

'Afghanistan, Peru, Turkey, Zimbabwe, India, Ecuador, Algeria. I'm meant to be in Colombia right now.'

Somehow, he was across the room. His body, usually excellent at doing exactly what he wished, had developed a mind of its own. He stood across from her. Close enough that he could reach out and brush his hand over her arm, down to that sweet hip of hers, squeezing her tight.

'Not exactly a Zagat guide of tourism hotspots for the average woman in her early twenties.'

'Unless you're into archaeology,' she pointed out.

'Where was your favourite?'

Her lips twisted. 'I couldn't choose.'

'You love what you do.' It was a statement; her passion was obvious. So too the heaviness of her sigh, when she looked up at him and nodded.

'Yes.'

Then he did reach out, surprising them both by putting a hand on her stomach. 'This isn't a death sentence, Rosemary. Our baby doesn't have to signal the end of your career.'

'That's actually more true now that I'm here with you than it was before.'

But he was hardly listening. He was a rational man, he knew it wasn't actually possible for their child to somehow be communicating with him, but the second his hand touched her stomach he felt the strangest aching sense of all-body warmth. It was as though he'd come home. It was overwhelmingly strange.

He pulled his hand back, dropping it to his side, keeping his gaze locked to a point above her head, rather than risking that she'd see whatever foolish emotions were rioting through him.

He wouldn't allow this baby to make him vulnerable.

'This is the guest suite of the apartment,' he said, glad

to be returning to a less personal topic of conversation. 'It was designed with groups of guests in mind. There are three bedrooms, each with their own bathroom, and there's a small private sitting room. I thought it would be perfect for you, a nursery and a nanny's room.'

'A nanny?' she repeated, and now his eyes did drop to hers, probing without meaning to, reading those green depths, and hating the way he was imagining their baby with her eyes and dimples.

'Do you have a problem with that?'

She twisted her hands in front of her in that way she had. It wasn't uncertainty so much as a placeholder, to indicate she was thinking something through.

'I guess it's way outside of my experience,' she said. 'Did you have a nanny?'

'Yes.'

She nodded, but he heard himself elaborating, for no reason he could think of. 'My mother was very hands-on, so my nanny—Marta—was with me if they travelled, or when they went out at night. She was an older woman from the village my mother grew up in. I sometimes wondered if my mother didn't take her on because she needed a job, and a home, after her own husband had died.'

Rosemary's smile changed her face completely. It was so unguarded and *beautiful*. So breathtakingly beautiful.

Out of nowhere, he remembered what it had been like, seeing her at the wedding. She'd been twenty. The teenager whose gaze had followed him around was nowhere in evidence. In her place had been a sinfully sexy, stunning Madonna, with her full breasts and dazzling smile. It was the kind of smile that changed her entire face, making her eyes sparkle and her cheeks glow.

He swallowed hard, forcing his body to heel, even when

it would have much preferred to keep exploring the connection they'd resurrected outside his mother's house.

'That sounds like your mum,' she said with obvious affection.

He felt a pang in his chest, but it was different to the jealousy he'd felt all those years earlier, when he'd been little more than a boy himself. At least, the motivation was different. He heard in Rosemary's voice an admiration for his mother that he knew she'd never feel for him.

And he didn't have to be a genius to work out why. From almost their first encounter, he'd treated her in a way that was designed to keep her at a distance. By belittling, rejecting, icing her out at every opportunity. He'd resented her place in his parents' life, but as she'd got older, and went from fourteen to eighteen, then nineteen, and grew into a woman, he'd started to resent the hold she had on him. He'd intentionally avoided conversations around her, left the room if his mother and father were discussing her archaeological studies, started planning his visits home around when she wouldn't be there. And in his absence she'd formed a connection with his mother that was real and full of love.

'I hate you.'

A salient reminder of her feelings for him, in total contrast to the way she was warmly reflecting on Melina.

'She has such a big heart. She didn't know anything about my family life, my mother, the way I was made to feel like an outsider in my own home,' she murmured. 'And yet it was like she did know. As though she just *understood.* She welcomed me with the kind of affection I'd never known.'

'I remember.'

Her eyes lifted to his, and that sweet smile slipped, smudging a thoughtful frown in its place. 'And you always hated me.'

Ice slid through his body. So too danger sirens. Because he wanted to deny that. To explain something he was only just starting to realise himself—how much more nuanced his response to her had been. How much it had been born from his own shocking discovery, and the difficulty he was having rediscovering his place in this life. He'd rejected her because of what he was going through; it was not—and never had been—about Rosemary.

All across Europe, he was the Machairas heir, the sole son of the great Stavros Machairas. But it was a lie. He was no more a Machairas than the next person. He'd been plucked from poverty and obscurity, chosen for some reason, by a twist of fate.

'I didn't hate you.'

'It's okay, I was used to it,' she quipped, but it made his insides catch fire with shame. He'd been navigating the emotional fallout of his adoption discovery, but Rosemary's life had hardly been a walk in the park. She'd been fought over and turned into a pawn in her parents' acrimonious divorce and then, when her mother remarried and had a new family, she'd been shunted to the side, made to feel like an encumbrance. And even then, her mother—who sounded like a selfish piece of work—hadn't been able to give her up, to let her live with Glen Richardson, because she'd still wanted to 'win'.

'It wasn't about you.'

Her hands twisted. 'No?'

'I hardly knew you,' he pointed out logically. 'You were just some teenager who appeared in my home.'

'Your mother told me I could go anywhere. I was too young to realise it was probably invasive of me to explore the way I did.'

'She told you to.'

She lifted one shoulder, her expression pinched. His gut felt hollowed out.

'I suppose even then I was fascinated by the past. I had never been somewhere like that. I mean, on class trips, to museums, but this was a living, breathing house that was so steeped in history. So casually available. In every room there were museum-worthy artefacts, paintings that could have been in the best galleries in the world. I would touch a wall and *feel* the past, pulsing and throbbing, just behind the veil. I could never reach through, but I could sense it, anyway.'

'I see,' was all he could say, because he could easily imagine how tantalizing that would have been for someone like Rosemary.

'I never said at the time how sorry I was, about your dad.'

It was like a gut punch. Not the statement—he'd heard that, or something like it, a thousand times. But from Rosemary's lips, with her soft, genuine voice, and the slight quiver in it showing that she felt those words deep in her heart. He almost reeled back physically. *'Your dad.'* But who was his dad? Who was he?

'He left me those encyclopaedias in his will, you know.'

Aristotle hadn't known. He hadn't thought about it.

'He knew how much I loved them,' she recalled a little wistfully. Then, with those intelligent, perceptive eyes latching to his, 'It must have been hard to see your mother move on so quickly.'

Another gut punch, but this time, the tone of the conversation had at least enabled him to brace for it.

'I was surprised.' Angry, disgusted, disbelieving.

'You and me both,' she said, shaking her head a little. 'I don't know how it happened.'

'Your father makes her happy,' he said after a beat.

'I know he respected your dad. I don't for one second think anything untoward was happening before he passed—'

'Nor do I.' He'd never once suspected it.

'Have you told her how you feel?'

He ground his teeth, surprised by the question. By what it suggested she understood about him. Ordinarily, he would have stepped away, but if anything, he seemed to move closer, without even realising he was doing it. He knew only that they were almost touching, chest to chest, toe to toe, so close he could feel a hint of her breath when she exhaled.

'How do I feel?'

'Hurt,' she said simply, looking at him as though she had no choice in the matter. As though the same invisible force that was propelling him forward was keeping her stuck in position.

'I am not hurt.' He heard the defensive ridicule in his tone, the cold rejection, and knew what underpinned it. A survival instinct. A desperate need to deny that anyone—even his own mother—had the ability to wound him now.

'Oh, sure,' she said, mockery clear in her tone. 'You're too big and tough to be hurt. I forgot.'

His eyes narrowed as his heart began to beat faster. There were parts of him he kept locked deep inside—even from himself—yet he couldn't help feeling that this woman was using her archaeological digging skills to discover them, completely without his consent.

'My mother is her own person,' he said, the words carefully blanked of feeling. 'She can do what she wants with her life.'

Rosemary's eyes narrowed, boring into his, leaving Aristotle with little doubt that she saw parts of him he didn't intend to share. And then, to his surprise—and relief—she lifted a hand to his chest, holding it against the middle of his pecs, palm pressed to the warmth of his shirt.

The response was instantaneous, as though she'd pressed a firecracker beneath his skin. Heat flooded his veins, then burst into every cell of his being. His eyes flared and his body hardened. As he sucked in a deep breath, his chest lifted, shifting her hand a little, but bringing his chest closer to her body.

Her tongue darted out, licking the middle of her lower lip, before disappearing again. But it was too late. His eyes were on her, staring. Hungry.

'I don't believe you,' she said slowly, and with a huskiness in her tone that told him that her control was hanging by a thread. That the same currents of desire that were flaring to life inside of him were burning through her, too.

'That's your prerogative.'

His response was guarded and cool, as though parts of his brain were still functioning, and actively pushing her away.

She glanced up at him, her expression flickering for a moment with sympathy. He tamped down on his irritation, but it was there. That sense that, yet again, she was scraping through the debris of his life to get to the core of who he was. And he wouldn't let her.

'I never asked why you were a virgin.'

It was a question that was designed to give him back the upper hand. To take control of a situation that was spiralling out of his control. But he hadn't expected how quickly she'd withdraw from him, dropping her hand and stepping back, so the heat he'd been flooded with quickly turned to ice—and regret.

'It hardly seems relevant.'

'Indulge me.'

Now it was Rosemary who was guarded, her features

pinched, as she visibly hid herself from him. 'I'd prefer not to.'

'You were twenty years old.'

'I remember.'

He took a step forward then, invading the space she'd sought. She held her ground, tilting her chin towards his. And as if he knew that he could seek refuge in the physicality of their connection, he reached out, pressing a finger to her cheek, watching the effect it had on her. The way her lips parted and her pupils darkened, the way her cheeks flushed pink and her breasts pushed forward almost imperceptibly, but enough to draw his attention. Briefly, lower, to notice the way her nipples were peaking against the flimsy material of her shirt.

'I touched you and you exploded,' he said, remembering that night. How he'd gone to tell her to steer clear of his 'friends', and ended up sleeping with her on the sofa in the study. Hardly the most salubrious environment for a woman's first time. Still, it had been better than the next time, hard up against a cold brick wall, with the party staff just a dozen or so metres across the property.

'And?'

He couldn't help but admire her. The way she stood there, staring back, giving as good as she got, not cowed by him. Most people came up against Aristotle and immediately bent to his will. Rosemary never had. Even with this wedding, he had no doubt she'd agreed because she could see the merits in it. Because she knew it was right for their baby, but also for herself, professionally.

'I just find it strange you'd never explored that.' His finger traced lower, towards her jaw, then tracked sideways, to the edge of her lips. Her eyes fluttered closed, giving him another visual clue as to how undone she was by this. Just like he was.

In the back of his mind, a voice was screaming at him, reminding him that this was stupid. That the stakes were so much higher for them now. There was a baby to think about; keeping this relationship impersonal and professional was essential. They were parenting partners, nothing more.

But the sparks igniting beneath his skin refused to be tamed.

He dropped his finger lower, to the jut of her decolletage and then with eyes that held hers, challenging her silently to stop him, to the curve of her breast, and inwards, to her nipple. She sucked in a sharp breath as he drew a circle around it, taking advantage of her sensory overload and stepping forward so his body could have what it craved—contact, from knees to hips, so his arousal was pressed close to her sex, leaving her with little doubt as to what he wanted.

And he did want.

No, he needed.

More than he'd needed before. Not just with Rosemary, but any woman. It was as though knowing they were going to be parents had added a great biological imperative to this, a sense that there was something bonding them that defied logic or sense, went deeper than pure physical connection.

A possessive need overtook him, so it wasn't enough to know that he'd been her first; he wanted to be her best. The only man who could drive her quite as wild, quite as fast.

His hand dropped from her breast, but only momentarily. Only so he could slide it beneath the stretchy material of her shirt, eyes locked to hers, as he pushed it higher, over her slightly rounded stomach, to the full swell of her breast and he groaned deeply when he felt the weight of it in his palm, so full and satisfying.

It was no longer enough to feel. He had to see.

'Take off your shirt,' he said. Commanding. No doubts. But in the back of his mind, he knew why he was telling her, rather than doing it himself. He needed her to buy into this. To prove to him that they were equally invested. He felt her tremble, noted the way she sucked her lower lip between her teeth, saw the way the hairs on her arms were standing on edge and understood, because he felt it too.

Her hands moved to the fabric far too slowly, so by the time she finally lifted it, he was almost exploding with impatience. Having slept with her twice, yet never seen her breasts, he was suddenly like a horny, inexperienced schoolboy, about to see a woman for the first time. What the hell was wrong with him?

Clamping his jaw, he nonetheless couldn't look away as she lifted the shirt from her head, then slid it down the side of her body, so it dropped to the floor with a soft rustle. Her bra was simple cotton. Nothing like the silky, lacy things he was used to seeing, and yet, the way her creamy breasts spilled at the top of it was the hottest thing he'd ever seen.

It was no longer enough to look. He needed to touch, taste, feel. To see and hold. His hand reached behind her, unclasping her bra swiftly, separating it so he could push the straps down her arms and remove the scrap of fabric. His eyes clung to hers as he did so, as his fingers ran over the soft, smooth skin, until the bra joined her shirt on the floor.

She trembled. Her nipples were a dusky pink colour, so perfect, so taut. As much as he wanted to drop his head and take one between his lips, then the other, he lifted both hands instead, cupping her breasts fully at first, and biting back a moan at the perfection of that.

'*Christós*,' he swore, though, because the sensual beauty of her body went straight to his cock, making him painfully hard, straining against the fabric of his pants. 'You are so damn beautiful,' he groaned, shaking his head with the sense that he was losing himself. Because this was *not* part of the plan. At no point, when he'd suggested marriage, had he thought there'd be a physical element to it. True, he hadn't exactly had time to concoct a plan for how to make it work, but Aristotle had been naïve not to think this issue might arise.

He dropped his head then, finally giving into his deep, dark desire and taking a nipple in his mouth, teasing it with his tongue at first, rolling it until she was whimpering and then sucking hard enough to make her jerk forward, hard, against him, her body like a livewire that only he could control.

'You are so perfect,' he said, moving his mouth to her other breast. 'I cannot believe we have slept together twice, and this is my first time seeing your breasts. Touching them like this.' He moved his hand to the nipple he'd just relinquished and squeezed it between his forefinger and thumb so she made a sound that was part yelp, part desperate, hungry cry for him.

He understood completely. There was a balance between them, of pleasure and pain, of need and knowledge: this was wrong, yet they couldn't stop it. And in that moment, all they could do was surrender, and deal with the aftermath in due course.

CHAPTER SEVEN

'*You are so perfect.*' She could only put it down to the sheer thickness of the sexual fog he'd created that it took her so long to process that compliment. To hear it and dismiss it. To hear it and be reminded of the lie that it was.

She was not perfect.

She was some woman he'd slept with on a dare, and then because—because why? Why had they slept together four months ago? Why had passion ignited like that? The first time had been one thing, but the second? And for neither to have thought of a condom?

But she couldn't let his praise stand unchallenged.

And she sure as hell couldn't let this happen again, no matter how much she wanted it. And she did. She wanted with a heat and need that was almost drugging. She wanted with every fibre of her being. She wanted him to take her, just like he had before, hard and fast, showing her that his body was not only the master of hers, but also completely enslaved to her. Showing her that he was as lost to this desperate heat as she was.

At what cost, though?

It wasn't as though they could sleep together and retreat to their separate corners of the globe, her disappearing on some dig and him going back to his take-no-prisoners approach to running his empire.

They were having a baby, and today they'd announced their engagement to Glen and Marina.

Sleeping together was the worst idea imaginable.

Say nothing of the fact that this man was someone she hated.

'No—' She wrenched her mouth free from his neck, where she'd been passionately kissing and tasting him, losing herself to the headiness of this moment. He pulled away instantly, looking at her with an expression that showed shock, and disbelief.

But he stopped at the first rejection from her, his body instantly stilling, with a willpower she recognised. Because the fog they were being swallowed by was intensely powerful.

'No,' she said again, as the certainty grew that she could never let this happen. It was for their baby, but it was also for her. 'I don't want this.'

He stood where he was, rigid and strong, arms crossed over his chest—which was moving hard with the rapid rise and fall of each breath—eyes boring into hers. His cheeks were slashed with dark colour, and she could see the wheels turning in his brain as he tried to get to grips with what was happening.

'Don't you?' he said finally, dropping his gaze to her breasts, pink from his ministrations, and positively aching for him to resume his attention. She couldn't fathom if his mouth or hands were more skilled, then decided it was the combination. The way he went from one to the other, stirring her effortlessly to a fever-pitch. Just like he always had.

She was so inexperienced, so quick to fall under his spell. It was mortifying. She reached down and scooped up her shirt, pulling it on, ignoring the fact she didn't fasten her bra in place, wishing she could ignore the way the fabric exacerbated the tingling of her nipples.

'You don't need to say that stuff,' she said, wishing her voice had emerged defiant instead of husky.

'What do you mean?'

'That I'm perfect, and beautiful.'

To his credit, he did an excellent job of looking genuinely confused.

'Okay. But why not?'

She compressed her lips as past hurt burst through her. Somehow, it was so much worse now, because of the situation they were in.

Back then, she'd taken the high road. She'd decided not to confront him, not to tell anyone about the dare. It had been easier to get on with her life, knowing she'd spent six years crushing on a guy who really wasn't worth the mud off her boots. Avoiding him was no longer an option, and suddenly, it made sense to just tell him what she thought of him, and why. At least then he'd get a clearer picture of why she hated him so much.

'Because I know why you slept with me, Aristotle.' The words slammed out of her mouth, angry and judgemental, loaded with the protective instincts she still felt for the twenty-year-old she'd once been.

His brows drew together.

'I heard your friends.'

Now his expression changed, briefly showing shock, before he wrestled it under control.

'What did you hear?'

She rolled her eyes. 'Spoken like someone with a guilty conscience. You want me to reveal what I heard before you admit how bad it was?'

'No, it was bad,' he surprised her by saying, eyes scanning her face.

'It was a dare,' she spat. 'You were dared to sleep with the chauffeur's daughter by your rich, snobby, awful friends. Even though I was so not your type. In fact, I was and am the polar opposite of your usual type. I guess you just hate to lose, and always did.'

He made a gruff, guttural sound then took a step towards her. She flinched, unable to bear the thought of him touching her.

'Why didn't you confront me about this then?'

'Why would I?'

'So I could damn well explain.'

'I didn't need an explanation. I heard it all. Including what you all thought of me. Which, in case you've forgotten, was definitely *not* perfect, and *not* beautiful.'

'What did you hear *me* say?' he demanded, hands thrust on his hips as he glared at her face. Her heart slammed into her ribs as she remembered his silence. She remembered digging her fingernails into her palms, desperately hoping he'd say something to defend her, to dispute the awful, vile ways in which they were referring to her.

'You just stood there, listening, while they laughed about me, asked if I was any good, said fat girls often were because they had to compensate for their looks with skills.'

He swore then, the colour draining from his face as he moved forward and wrapped his hands around her upper arms.

'You didn't defend me,' she said, shaking her head. 'I mean, I don't know why that surprised me. I don't know why that *hurt* me. I guess I just loved your mother so much, I saw the best in you, even when you didn't deserve it. Still, I never expected—'

'I did defend you,' he disputed with quiet strength. 'In fact, that conversation, that night, was the last time I saw any of those people. I told them to leave the house and never return. Whatever else you were, you became family that night—at least, to my mother. I was not about to let them disrespect you in those terms.'

She blinked away the sting of tears before ripping out of his hands. 'I don't believe you.'

'Listen to me.'

She didn't want to. She didn't want to give him any room to wiggle back into something like her good books. Hating him was safe. Being angry with him important.

'Listen to me,' he said again. Deeper, darker, with more urgency, and she made the mistake of glancing in his direction and seeing the raw, obvious desperation in his features. She sucked in an uneven breath, pressing her teeth into her lower lip to stem the threat of tears.

'I did not sleep with you because of a dare.'

'I heard—'

'I don't know what you heard,' he interrupted, slashing a hand through the air. 'It was not a dare, but a game.'

The world seemed to tilt cruelly off-balance. She reached around for something to support her, finding nothing. And then, Aristotle was there, his hands on her hips ballasting her against the storm that was to follow.

'A game?' she whispered, eyes sweeping shut.

'It started that night, after the wedding. God, but you were beautiful, Rosemary. So real and womanly, all curves and creamy skin, so luscious…'

'Luscious?' she said with a roll of her eyes, inwardly disputing his description.

'They noticed. But you're right, they were snobs. It became a running joke, that you were the chauffeur's daughter, that the chauffeur was my new father. It was insensitive and cruel on every level.'

A tear slid down her cheek. She angled her face to hide it from him, lips wobbling.

'They put money down on who could sleep with you that night. When I came to you, it was to warn you to stay away from them. I planned to go from you to them, to tell them to get the hell out. I don't know what happened. The next minute, we were kissing, and then making love. I was completely unprepared for it. I didn't come to you planning to sleep with you, Rosemary. It was…out of my control.'

Her eyes swept shut then on a wave of feeling. She was so confused. On the one hand, everything he was saying seemed plausible. It certainly fitted the idea she had of his character far more than the thought of him having sex with her on a dare.

'Someone said something about money,' she murmured.

He made a groaning noise. 'There was a prize pool.'

She swore then, under her breath, feeling dirty all over. 'Disgusting men.'

'Yes.'

She looked up at him then, frowning. 'Did you really kick them out?'

'Yes.'

'But I heard them, and you were there. I stood there for a full minute, listening to the way they spoke about me, the things they said, and you were silent.'

'I was silent because it was taking absolutely every ounce of my self-control not to punch each and every one of them in the smug face. I abhor that sort of sexist, degrading treatment of women. Those friendships were formed out of time and place, but they were never men I particularly respected.

Until that night, though, I had not realised what they were capable of.'

He lifted his hands then, cupping her cheeks. 'I am mortified to think you have carried this opinion for four years. To know that you believed me capable of that, Rosemary.' He ran the pad of his thumb over her cheek, the soft flesh there, catching a tear and smudging it into oblivion.

'It was the logical assumption.'

He nodded once, but she could see the hint of betrayal in his eyes. She'd really surprised him with the accusation.

'You'd never looked at me before.'

'You came to the wedding a woman,' he said simply. 'From the moment you walked in and I saw you, I wanted you. I think there probably wasn't a single man in that room who didn't feel as I did.'

She rolled her eyes then. 'No need to gild the lily, Aristotle. I meant what I said before. I'm nothing like the women you usually sleep with.'

A muscle jerked at the base of his jaw. 'No, you're not. You're nothing like anyone I've ever known. My God, Rosemary, do you have any idea what I want to do with you? You fill my dreams, my thoughts; I have never touched a woman and felt like I would die if I couldn't possess her in that precise moment. How else do you explain this?' he asked, gesturing to her stomach.

She sucked in a sharp breath, unable to speak because of the strength of his words.

Then, he was dropping his hands, taking a step back, visibly drawing himself together, resuming a mask of control.

'Which is precisely why we have to be more careful.'

She blinked at him, almost suffering from whiplash, courtesy of the shift in his demeanour.

'Nothing about this changes what we are, and what we

want. We're getting married for the sake of our baby, for the kind of parents we want to be, the life we want to give them.' He hesitated a moment before narrowing his gaze, and seemingly firming up on his commitment. 'Sex has the potential to complicate this. When I proposed, I didn't envisage this becoming physical, and I think it's best if we hold to that. No matter how tempted we are. It doesn't make sense to muddy these waters for a temporary satisfaction.'

A lump in her throat made it hard to swallow, but she nodded quickly. In her heart of hearts, she knew he was right.

'Good.' He took a step backwards then, further getting control of himself in a way she could physically see. 'I'll have a decorator I know come by tomorrow to discuss colours, and any other changes you'd like to make. We should start selecting nursery furniture as well. My mother informs me these things can take time to arrive.'

It was so matter-of-fact, so businesslike, that it left her reeling, but she nodded anyway, suddenly needing, more than anything, to be left alone. She felt bruised all over and on fire at the same time.

When she didn't answer, he offered a curt half-smile in her direction and left the room, so Rosie was left staring at a void where he'd just been.

Weirdly, it was one of the best sleeps Rosie could remember. She was exhausted after the tumult of the day before. From Aristotle showing up on her doorstep, it had been an out-of-control whirlwind, culminating in that sensually charged moment last night. In this very room.

Her eyes strayed to the space they'd occupied, when he'd asked her to take off her shirt *and she'd done it*. Even now, her nipples felt sensitive, aching for his touch.

'Sex has the potential to complicate this.'

Yes.

It did.

He was completely right. She rolled onto her side, one hand wrapping around her stomach while she lifted the other in front of her and stared at the engagement ring. She knew pregnancy could make your emotions riot, but there was another explanation for the way she felt this morning.

Lightness.

Relief.

Because the facts of that night, four and a half years earlier, were different to what she'd thought. He hadn't slept with her on a dare, and he *had* stuck up for her. Or he'd struck out against the sexual, misogynistic treatment of women generally, but because of how his friends had spoken to her.

She'd been carrying around a lump of hatred for the man she'd lost her virginity to, and it wasn't warranted. At least, not in that respect. She hadn't fully realised how much that belief had been hurting her until she was relieved of the burden.

He was still a man who'd strong-armed her into agreeing to marry him, though, using their child as a bargaining chip. Except even then, she found it hard to feel angry with him, because she genuinely believed he was doing what he believed was right for their child. As was she.

Rosie stretched in the luxuriously comfortable bed, the crisp sheets like something one might find in the best hotel in the world, all starchy but comfortable, and sat up, looking around the room with renewed interest, and then gave a small half-smile to see her faithful suitcase in the corner. It looked like it belonged in this apartment about as much as she did, which was to say, not at all.

No matter. When she was done with this place, nothing

but the view and the plush bed would be the same. If she was going to marry Aristotle, and live here in Athens with him, then she was going to turn this apartment into the kind of nest she wanted to raise her baby in.

There wasn't a moment to lose.

Aristotle was standing over the coffee machine when she padded into the kitchen a short while later, staring at it as though he was disappointed it wasn't producing his morning brew fast enough.

He glanced up when she entered, and the way his gaze quickly ran over her made her glad she'd got dressed. The simple cotton nightshirt she slept in left little to the imagination. Up until last night, she would have said that didn't matter—as if Aristotle would notice—but she had proof, and knowledge now, to the contrary.

'How did you sleep?'

Her lips tugged into another small smile. 'Like a baby.' Her hand pressed over her stomach. 'That bed should be illegal. It's so comfortable.'

His eyes narrowed imperceptibly. 'I'm glad. Coffee?'

She nodded. 'I'd kill for one.'

He slid a cup into the machine and pressed the button. 'How do you take it?'

'White, no sugar.'

He strode to the fridge, and her eyes did their own unapproved inspection, slipping from his face to his broad shoulders, narrow waist and strong legs. He wore a suit, but no socks or shoes, and her heart did a funny little leap at the sight of his bare feet.

Which was ridiculous.

She'd seen bare feet before.

She'd seen *his* bare feet before.

A memory seared her, catching her completely by surprise and driving the breath from her body. Aristotle, one summer, striding out to the pool where she'd been reading *The Travels of Marco Polo*. He'd barely even glanced in her direction but she—at sixteen—had practically burned him into her retinas. She'd never known anyone like him in the real world. Her boarding school was female only, and when she did socialise with boys, they were smaller. Paler. More two-dimensional. Aristotle was all shimmering gold, Greek god Adonis, and in that moment he'd been stripped down to a pair of black swimming trunks that showed his lithe athleticism and sculpted masculinity to perfection.

She'd practically drooled into her medieval book.

'Rosemary.' His voice had a hard edge, a sharp current of warning in the syllables of her name.

She forced her eyes to drag back to his face, only to realise she'd been caught shamelessly staring. And probably drooling again.

Yes, he'd clearly caught her. Heat flamed in her face.

His chest moved with the force of his exhalation.

'There are some things we need to discuss. Everything happened very quickly yesterday, but now that you're here, and the dust has settled, we can start working out the logistics of all this.'

'Yes,' she said. 'I was just reflecting to myself about what a whirlwind yesterday was.'

He added the milk to a jug and began to froth it with all the skill of an actual barista. She stared at his hands, fascinated by the way he held the jug, fingers so confident as he swirled it around. Then, she wasn't seeing his hands on the jug, but rather on her breasts, the contrast of his dark brown skin against her creamy fair skin, the way it had struck her that they were so different, even then.

Her lips parted as her breasts tingled, as though trying to beg him to not only notice them, but also to touch them. They were aching for his attention, just as they had been in bed this morning. She glanced away, but not before her eyes skated upwards and found him looking at her, a small frown etched on his face.

'I have a meeting this morning. I would reschedule it, but the King of Al Anja is flying in particularly for it. Shall we say lunch?'

She tried not to look disconcerted by the fact he was casually mentioning a meeting with one of the most powerful royals in the world. It wasn't Al Anja's royal family's wealth she was thinking of, though, but their treasure trove of historical sites.

'Have you ever been?' she asked, as he handed the coffee over to her.

He raised a brow.

'To Al Anja,' she elaborated.

'Yes.' He sipped his own coffee—a short black—in one sip. 'Have you?'

'Three times.' She sighed. 'It's an incredible country. I could lose myself in their history. So much culture and tradition, such incredible artefacts. My second dig was there.'

'Where exactly?'

'The mountains to the west—the tomb of Akhamandi.'

'I haven't heard of it.'

'I'm not surprised. He was just a village leader from the second century BC. Lost, really, to obscurity and time, except for the fact his tomb was so excellently preserved. The things we uncovered there, and what they told us about daily life…'

She tapered off to find his eyes roaming her face, an expression on his own she couldn't interpret.

'You love what you do.'

She sipped her coffee, nodding once. 'Yes.'

'This is something we have to discuss. I have no intention of allowing our baby to prevent you from following your dreams.'

She ignored the way her heart warmed at that. But, in truth, it had been one of her primary considerations, and concerns, since discovering her pregnancy. She'd never planned on having children, mainly because she'd never wanted to get involved with someone, knowing that it could lead to the sort of acrimonious marriage breakdown she'd witnessed between her parents. From the moment she'd known about her little baby on board, she'd known it closed the door on a lot of the fieldwork she relished.

'So, lunch?'

She nodded once.

His eyes, obsidian black, seemed to shimmer like a gemstone. 'I'll have my assistant send a car.'

CHAPTER EIGHT

SHE HAD KNOWN Aristotle Machairas in his family home, and the context of his mother and father. In that ancient, expansive property, he had been simply a part of it, like a thread of a tapestry, albeit a shimmery gold one that couldn't fail to catch her eye.

Here, against the glittery backdrop of this clearly exclusive and ritzy restaurant, she realised he was so much more, to so many people.

He was Aristotle Machairas.

Titan of industry.

Powerhouse investor.

Greek god billionaire.

In his late twenties and one of the wealthiest men in the world, mostly through his own guile and genius. He was revered, respected and drooled over by almost everyone in the restaurant—men and women equally. These were his people. This was his life.

And the warm pleasure Rosie had felt that morning evaporated completely, leaving her with a very familiar sense of not belonging. Certainly not with Aristotle.

The dress she'd chosen to wear hid her pregnancy curves, the way her breasts had grown bigger by a size already and her stomach rounded, her hips already seeming to have swelled out, and she'd thought she looked quite nice before leaving the apartment, with her auburn hair brushed and curled loosely and a dash of make-up on her face to add colour. But here, surrounded by reed-thin women dripping in diamonds and couture, with handbags that probably cost more than she earned in a summer, she felt something she hadn't really known since her father's wedding.

That night, she'd sworn she would never again let anyone make her feel less than. Make fun of her. Take away her confidence. Yet here she was, sitting opposite Aristotle with a sense that he should be with any number of the women in this place. Not her.

'How was your meeting?' she asked, hardly able to meet his eyes as she reached instead for her mineral water, running a finger down the condensation at the side before lifting the glass to her lips and taking a sip. Then almost spitting it out when she caught the intensity of his gaze on her mouth. It felt almost obscene. Even more so when she lifted a finger and wiped at the corner of her lip, where a small droplet of water had landed.

His cheeks slashed with dark colour and beneath the table, he shifted his legs. Not intentionally to touch her, she was sure, given his determined boundary setting the night before, but nonetheless, his foot brushed against hers, and then his knee hit her knee, and she was ready to weep for how much she wanted him.

Common sense be damned.

'Aristotle?' she prompted, when the silence between them had grown thick and the air seemed to crackle with electricity, so she wasn't sure how either of them could move without getting shocked.

His brow furrowed into a deeper frown. 'Fine.'

'Fine?'

‘Are you interested in my work?’

She pulled a face. ‘Would you prefer me not to be?’ After all, they weren’t friends, they weren’t a couple.

He contemplated that, and beneath the table, she fidgeted with her fingers.

‘It’s not something I generally discuss with the women I date. Then again, we’re not dating.’

She ignored the various little darts of pain buried in those sentences. His casual reference to other women—and of course, there’d been many. His quick reminder that this wasn’t a date. If anything, it was another business meeting. Thinking of it in that context would be helpful for Rosie. She had to ignore the buzzing and crackling she felt and focus on the conversation they needed to have. Because he was right. There was so much to discuss.

‘That’s fine,’ she said, ignoring the flicker of curiosity inside of her, because she really did want to know how it had gone, and what he was working on with the King. But boundaries were important, and would protect both of them. ‘I was just making conversation. It’s better to stick to our own business.’

Despite her best efforts, she knew her voice emerged strained. Hurt. She wasn’t as good at covering that as she’d have liked, but so what? She doubted Aristotle noticed. A moment later, a waiter appeared to take their order, giving her vital minutes to compose herself as she quickly scanned the menu and selected a moussaka with twice baked potatoes on the side.

‘I’m hungry,’ she explained, cheeks flushing as she tried not to imagine the sort of food his dates usually ordered.

He only nodded distractedly, then templed his fingers beneath his chin, regarding her thoughtfully.

‘Let’s talk about our marriage,’ he said. Simply. Easily.

As though they were discussing the public transport system, or travel plans.

She nodded though, taking another sip of her mineral water.

'I think we should establish some ground rules around our relationship.'

She arched a brow. 'What relationship?'

'Exactly.'

'You don't like me,' she said, lifting one shoulder, ignoring the dull pain in the middle of her chest. 'You never have.'

He leaned back in his chair a little, those dark eyes resting on her face in a way she found disconcerting. 'I barely know you.'

She glanced down at the table, swallowing. Strangely, she couldn't say the same. 'It's funny, I feel like I know you, even though we haven't spent much time together. Your parents always talked about you.'

She *felt* him stiffen. It was impossible. They weren't touching, and yet the air around them seemed to change, to grow thick and heavy all of a sudden.

'They talked about you, too,' he said finally, a reserve in his voice that she didn't understand. Was it her relationship with his parents? Or the fact they'd spoken about her? 'My mother said she'd never known anyone quite so curious as you.'

'Curious?' she repeated, shaking her head.

'Asking questions. Exploring. Wanting to understand everything about the world.'

She wrinkled her nose. 'They were always so good to me.'

She glanced up at him, felt the heat in his gaze and looked away quickly. The restaurant was busy, and the conversations of the other diners formed a background hum that should have been relaxing. It wasn't. Or maybe that was sitting across from Aristotle like this. Rosie was aware, the entire time, of the stretching of her nerves like fine wires being pulled impossibly taut, so she found it hard to think of anything other than the fact she could shift her legs beneath the table and brush against him once more.

'In terms of our marriage,' he said, tone businesslike. 'We should see it more as a partnership.'

Her stomach clenched.

'A business arrangement,' he clarified. 'With defined boundaries and expectations. Our shared interest is our child. We'll work as a team to make sure he or she has the best possible life.'

It all sounded so reasonable, but in the back of her mind she couldn't help but see wrinkles in this very sterile imagining of a marriage.

'How will it work?' she asked, looking for reassurance, so she could share his sense of confidence.

'The more professional we keep it, the better,' he said. 'Obviously, in certain situations, there'll be an element of make-believe—'

'Like when we're with my dad and your mother.'

He dipped his head in silent agreement.

'And what about when we're with our child?'

'I don't understand.'

She compressed her lips, fingers twisting in the fabric of the tablecloth, where it draped against her knees. 'Well, don't you think our son or daughter will think it's strange that we're married, but not a couple?'

'Children accept whatever reality they're presented with.'

That was true.

'We will not be unhappy, Rosemary. Our child will grow up in a calm household, with two parents who take care of them, and look after their best interests.'

She bit into her lip. More sterile, bland descriptors. She couldn't help but wonder what was beneath the surface of that. 'What was your childhood like?'

'Is that relevant?' That same stiffness was back in his voice, reminding her forcibly of the closing of a drawbridge.

'Yes.'

He kept his expression neutral, silently waiting for her to elaborate.

'We're going to be raising a child together,' she said on a half laugh. 'I think our own experiences are deeply relevant—they shape the kind of parents we'll be.'

'You saw my childhood.'

'You were grown-up by the time I started coming to Greece.'

'But it was much like you experienced,' he said, slightly exasperated. 'I had the run of the estate, time and freedom to explore. I was less interested in history,' he added unnecessarily. 'For me, it was more about hiking.'

'Hiking?'

'I'd walk for hours. Down the hill, towards the city, picking my way through the wooded area of the property.'

'You went to school in Athens?'

He nodded once.

'And that's where you'd want our child to attend?'

There was a reserve in his face then, a flick of his lips. 'My preference would be the opposite.'

'You didn't like it?'

'I think we have to take care to choose a school with peers who are not so entitled as my cohort was.'

It reminded her swiftly of the friends who'd come to the wedding, who'd treated her so awfully.

'Yes,' she said, nodding. 'You're right. So then, how do we decide that sort of thing?'

'As I said, we're a partnership. We talk it through, weigh up options, and so long as we keep our child's best interests front and centre, and let that guide us, we'll make good choices.'

He was so confident that this could be a calm, dispassionate arrangement, that sitting here across from him she almost forgot the elephant in the room. Then he shifted so his foot accidentally brushed her calf, and flames ignited once more, threatening to torch the whole damn world.

His pragmatic approach to this marriage lasted three days. He was able to exist in his suite of rooms at the penthouse, conscious that Rosemary was upstairs in her own suite, but not altering his day-to-day life to factor her in. Though there were signs of her occupancy in the shared spaces—herbal tea bags and pregnancy multivitamins were lined up on the kitchen counter. Some brightly coloured cushions had found their way into the starkly monochromatic living room, and there was a well-thumbed paperback novel on an occasional table. The grand piano that had come with the penthouse had been played, going by the lifted lid.

He moved to it and pressed a key, closing his eyes as the dark, deep note hit him, like a sledgehammer.

He hadn't stopped to think since he'd learned of her pregnancy.

He'd acted purely on instinct, knowing that he would move heaven and earth to claim his child. To make the sort of choices that would lead his baby to grow up knowing they were wanted. Unlike Aristotle had felt because of his birth parents' rejection.

He pressed the key again, harder this time.

The marriage contracts were ready to be signed. His lawyers had drafted a thorough agreement, covering every contingency. From divorce to his death, to dispute resolution within their marriage, to their decision-making process for things such as education and health. It was balanced and fair.

Practical.

Just as their marriage would be.

He pressed the key again, ignoring the memories that were swirling through him. The feel of her soft, petal-like skin. The taste of her mouth. The sounds she made when he kissed her.

But the memories were too strong, swirling fiercely, so he smothered a groan as he stepped away from the piano and moved back to the table, where he'd placed the paperwork upon arriving home.

He'd get Rosemary to sign these tonight. It would be a powerful reminder—that he suddenly seemed to desperately need—that this was just like any other business deal.

'*Christós*—what in God's name do you think you are doing?'

His voice was a growl that seemed to bounce around the walls of the soon-to-be-nursery. She gripped the top of the ladder before turning to face him, ignoring the way her protective mask made her nose itch. Hating the way her body responded to his instantly. But it had been three days, and she hadn't seen nor heard him. He worked long hours, she gathered, and by the time she went to the kitchen to make toast and coffee in the mornings, he was usually gone. As for the nights, she had been spending a lot of time *not* thinking about where he was, who he was with, because none of that was her business.

'What do you mean?'

He walked quickly towards her, hands gripping the bottom of the ladder. 'Why the hell are you up a ladder?'

She stared at him as though he'd lost his mind. 'Well,

I couldn't think of another way to reach the top,' she explained. 'Do you like the colour?'

He didn't take his eyes off her. His expression was *furious*. 'Get down, now.'

Her jaw dropped, making the mask itch more. 'Why are you shouting at me?'

'Because you're pregnant with my baby and you're perilously high up a ladder, painting some wall that I would have had painted for you.'

Irritation made her snappy, but she bit back her first response, instead, doing as he'd commanded and gradually coming down from the ladder, paintbrush held between her finger and thumb. At the bottom of the steps, she placed it on the paint can lid, then brushed her hands over her old jeans—they still fitted, so long as she didn't attempt to marry the button to its hole.

'I'm pregnant with *our* baby,' she said, when she could trust her voice to emerge calmly. 'And I'm more than capable of climbing a ladder.'

'I organised a decorator,' he said, shaking his head.

A shiver ran down Rosie's spine. The decorator had been a fabulously elegant woman in her twenties, who was no doubt very good at her job. She was also cut from the exact same cloth as his 'friends' had been. Entitled, arrogant, condescending. She'd taken one look at Rosie and sneered her way through the meeting.

'I decided to do it myself.' She shrugged, removing her mask and dropping it to the ground. It was a precaution she hadn't needed to take, strictly speaking. The guy at the hardware store had assured her the paint was non-toxic, but it was proof of how seriously she was taking their baby's safety. 'I need a project.'

'You are *not* to climb that ladder again.'

She glared at him, anger sparking in her chest. Or perhaps it was repressed need, because it had been three days without an Aristotle sighting, and now her body was exploding with the force of their chemistry. Why was it like this between them?

'*You* are not to tell me what to do,' she returned, jabbing her finger into his chest for good measure.

His nostrils flared as he expelled an angry breath. 'You are so unreasonable.'

'Hello, pot, kettle, black. You literally just stormed in here and started shouting at me. But *I'm* the unreasonable one?'

'You can't be surprised I'm annoyed.'

'You have no reason—no, no right—to be annoyed at me. I'm not your property. I'm not your employee. You don't get to control me.'

He held up a stack of paper. 'This gives me the right.'

She blanched.

'Not to control you,' he contradicted, shaking his head angrily. 'But to demand you behave reasonably.'

'Do you hear yourself?' She jammed a hand onto her hips, glaring up at him. 'What the hell, Aristotle?'

'What? I'm not allowed to feel protective of our baby?'

Her hand pressed to her stomach, and despite his macho bullshit she couldn't help but feel a weird heartwarming at that. *'Our baby'*. She wasn't alone in this, and the love she felt for this little person was shared completely by the man opposite her.

'You don't need to protect our baby from me.'

'You are not to climb that ladder again.'

She gestured to the wall, which was half painted. 'Well, I'm not leaving it like this, sooo…'

'I'll do it.'

She rolled her eyes. 'I *like* painting. I'm enjoying myself. I've been doing this for three days, you know,' she said.

Aristotle's expression shifted and then he turned on his heel and stalked from the room. She followed him, wondering if he was actually walking away from her. But no.

He went to the spare room first, shaking his head and smothering what she suspected was a curse as he took in the pale lemon colour she'd painted the walls, to complement the creamy white office furniture she'd bought. Rather than using the space for a nanny, she'd set it up as a workspace. With a single disapproving glance in her direction, he moved back out of the door and into her bedroom.

The breath hissed out of his lungs as he did a slow pivot, eyes tracing all the changes. She'd been busy, but she'd had to be.

Pregnancy had made her restless, and though she was still months from giving birth, those nesting instincts were strong. There was no way she could 'nest' in the sterile environment it had been. The walls in here were a deep, dark pink, luxurious and feminine, and she'd chosen a sumptuous floral duvet set and accessorized it with fluffy cream cushions. She'd bought a moss-green chair—velvet, with rockers—for the corner, keeping in mind the inevitable future of late-night feeds of their baby.

He turned to face her, lips compressed. She couldn't tell what he was thinking. His expression was dark, though. 'You did this yourself?'

'I had the furniture delivered,' she said.

'But the painting?'

She nodded. 'And lived to tell the tale.'

He shook his head, but whatever anger he'd felt in the baby's room was kept at bay. He shifted his attention back to her room, completing another slow inspection, eyes raking over all the details, including the small collection of books that went everywhere with her.

'I know, it's very different to what was here…'

He was silent.

'You did say I could make any changes I wanted.' Her voice was defensive to her own ears. 'Didn't you?'

Aristotle turned back to her then, his expression taut, his body tense.

'What the hell is going on with you?' she demanded then, stalking across the room and standing toe to toe with him, ignoring the way her stomach rolled when she caught a hint of his masculine fragrance.

'I don't know,' he said finally, darkly, angrily, shaking his head, before putting his hands on her forearms and pulling her towards him. 'I never know with you, Rosemary, and I hate that.'

The words were swallowed by his desperate, hungry kiss.

CHAPTER NINE

THE VOICE IN the back of his mind wasn't subtle. It wasn't a whisper. It was a shout. Over and over, telling him to *stop*.

Kissing Rosemary was not the solution here. It was something he'd sworn they wouldn't do. Couldn't do. It threatened everything he'd predicated this marriage gambit on—that they could approach the raising of their child as two calm, sensible adults, doing what was right for their baby, without letting anything physical get in the way.

It was supposed to be neat. Clean.

Not messy.

But this…it was impossible to fight it. Not right now.

From the second he'd seen her up that ladder, a fuse had been lit. It had emerged as anger, but it had taken seeing this room to understand that it was so much more complicated. This room that she'd somehow transformed into a physical embodiment of *herself.* It was all lush, soft, feminine and tactile, a space that practically screamed Rosemary Richardson, and all he could think was that he had to make her his. To make her his in a way he'd never done, because the previous two times they'd slept together had been quick and desperate. He hadn't worshipped her body as she deserved. He hadn't taken the time to sink into the experience of being with her.

And he shouldn't now.

He really shouldn't.

'Tell me to stop,' he heard himself ask, tone raspy, pleading with her to be the voice of reason in the midst of this maelstrom.

She pulled back from him, eyes meeting his, cheeks flushed, lips full and dark from the pressure of his kiss. He lifted his thumb and ran it over her lower lip, insides lurching with heat and need.

'Damn it, Rosemary, we shouldn't do this.'

She nodded, eyes probing his. 'I know,' she said, and he closed his eyes, hating that she was going to do what he'd asked, and put an end to it.

'It's not like we haven't had sex before, you know,' she said, surprising him by putting her hand on his chest and grabbing his shirt. 'And it's not as if pretending each other doesn't exist is making us want this less…'

The fuse was almost at its end, about to explode. He ground his teeth, willing himself to find some kind of sense in this situation.

'Maybe what we need is to sleep together properly, and get it out of our systems,' she said, lifting one shoulder, drawing his attention first there, and then lower, to the way her breasts rose and fell with each breath.

His arousal strained painfully against his trousers. It wasn't the sense he'd been looking for, but it was a reasonable enough explanation. It was something he could take hold of and cling to.

'I mean, don't you think that's what's going on here?' she prompted, her hand making small half-circles over his chest. 'We just have pent-up sexual energy, because of the whole forbidden fruit thing.'

Yes. Forbidden fruit. That was exactly what Rosemary

was—and always had been. He should have known better than to give in to temptation the night of his mother's wedding. But she'd been so beautiful and, much like now, he'd been completely powerless to resist.

It was not a sensation he enjoyed—powerlessness. He liked control. Predictability. He liked the certainty that the relationships in his life were as expected, because he'd had the rug pulled out from under him once before, and it had changed everything he thought he knew about the world.

'It's just sex,' he heard himself say, desperately trying to find his control in the midst of this mess. 'It doesn't change anything between us.'

She rolled her eyes upwards. 'Obviously.'

Despite the undercurrent of need that was vibrating inside of him, he smiled at her quick, condescending rejoinder. If possible, he'd found someone who was even more averse to the idea of a happy ending than he was. Someone who felt every bit as cynical about the safety and security of relationships as him.

Someone for whom sex really could just be sex.

'Fuck it,' he groaned, dragging her against him, his body rejoicing in the promise of what was to come. 'Let's get it out of our system, Rosemary, and then we can move on with our lives.'

'Yes,' she agreed quickly, pushing up onto the tips of her toes and kissing him with the same passion that was threatening to burn him to the ground.

Except even then, as they made that simplistic agreement and promise, from the second he felt her breasts in his hands, he knew it wouldn't be quite that easy. Rosemary was not someone you simply 'got out of your system'. She was addictive.

If he'd been thinking, he might have come to the wise conclusion that making love to her would only make him want her more, not less, but he was clutching at the straw she'd offered, clinging to the idea that exposure therapy would cure him of his insatiable need.

She was so soft, so curvaceous. His hands roamed her body like a starving man brought to a banquet. Though he'd told himself he'd go slowly, and relish the discovery of her properly this time, in reality, his desperation wouldn't allow it. He tore at her clothes impatiently, needing to feel her nakedness, to see all of her, and she wrenched his shirt with the same motivation, pushing the buttons apart, and with an impatient growl in his mouth he continued to kiss her like his life depended on it.

The first time they'd had sex, she'd been a virgin. He hadn't known it, but if he'd been less senseless with desire, he might have noticed a timidity to her touch, a trembling in her fingers as she'd tentatively traced them across his shoulders and down his back. The opposite could be said of her tonight. Now, she touched him as though she couldn't not, her hands brushing his arms, his back, his chest as though she too was desperate to commit this to memory.

Then she ripped her mouth from his, her breath rushed, as she dropped her lips to his chest and feathered kisses across him, from one nipple to the other, so he groaned and lifted her easily, carrying her across to the sumptuous floral bed and laying her down on it. He pulled back to stare at her, needing a moment.

It was such a powerfully moving sight. The woman he was to marry, who was carrying his baby, almost naked, against the backdrop of a floral bedspread. She was so incredibly feminine, he almost couldn't bear it.

But something shifted in her features, a look of uncertainty. Insecurity?

Anger flared to life inside of him, because he knew why. Her first experience with him might have been satisfying, but for four years afterwards she'd believed that he'd only had sex with her because his stupid friends had put him up to it. The opposite was true, and now he had a chance to show her how desirable she was.

'You are perfect,' he said, shaking his head as he brought his body over hers and kissed her mouth once more, his hands resuming their exploration of her body before sliding into the cotton of her underpants and pushing them down. He had to break the kiss to complete the job, but he made lemonade out of lemons and dragged his mouth down her body, over her breasts, her gently rounded stomach, and finally, to her sex.

She cried his name into the room and he smiled against her, the craving in her voice something he could get used to. Particularly knowing that it was because of him.

'Please...' she whimpered, twisting her beautiful hips on the bed, driven wild by need, so he focused on her most sensitive cluster of nerve-endings until she was coming apart against his mouth, in a flurry of cries and sounds that resembled words but weren't quite.

And then Aristotle stood, moving to his discarded trousers, removing his wallet and retrieving a condom. Her eyes fell to the small silver square.

'Don't you think that's a little redundant now?' she asked through spurts of breath, as the pleasure waves still ran through her body.

He considered that. She was right in terms of pregnancy, but there were other reasons to wear one.

'You are the only person I've ever had unprotected sex with,' he said, knowing that he was clean.

She nodded. 'Same.'

He dropped the condom to the floor, suddenly hungry beyond bearing to take her and make her his. To feel himself buried inside her, with no barrier between them whatsoever, just as it had been last time. But so much better now, because this wouldn't be rushed. It wouldn't be against a damn wall.

He strode towards the bed, then froze at the foot of it, staring down at this woman as a thousand kaleidoscope images filtered through his mind, reminding him forcibly of *who* she was. Not just the woman he was going to marry for the sake of their baby. But a woman he'd known for a long time. Who was beloved by his mother. Who could see through him and read him like a book. A woman he had to be careful not to let close—he'd always known that about her. He'd always felt the danger she posed, with those assessing eyes and thoughtful face. But she was also a woman he couldn't ever hurt.

The stakes were too high, the consequences too real.

'Rosemary—' he said, but she lifted her hand then, reaching for his, pulling at him to join her, and every presentiment of disaster was instantly dispelled. They were two consenting adults and they knew what they were doing.

Sleeping together to get rid of this electrical storm of desire, once and for all.

The first time he'd made love to her had woken Rosie up to the concept of sexual pleasure. It had rocked her world, in fact. The second time had been so much more, because she had no longer been a virgin. She'd been as much in control as him.

But *this* was completely different.

He pushed into her slowly at first, eyes watching hers, as he braced himself over her, so her whole skin seemed to burst with the heat of the sun and her body felt tingly all over. Air hissed from beneath her teeth as he moved deeper, and deeper, and finally, hitched himself all the way in, so she let out a slow moan as her muscles tightened and expanded to cope with his impressive size.

'You feel so good, Rosemary. You're so tight.' His voice was more accented than normal, deep and husky. She could listen to him sounding like that all night.

She arched her back, riding the wave of euphoria that ebbed through her with the completeness that she felt in this moment. The sense that this was just exactly as it was meant to be.

He pulled out a little, so she dug her fingernails into his shoulder and he laughed, a deep husky sound that seemed to fill the room.

'Please,' she groaned, tilting her hips.

He drove into her, and she cried out. This time, there was nothing gentle or slow about his invasion. It was designed to shock and please, to bring her to a fever-pitch. Stars seemed to burst in her eyes.

'Aristotle—' she groaned, his name like a spell in her mouth, a magical incantation that seemed to echo with the fractured fullness of all the time that had gone before.

Then speech was impossible.

Thinking was a lost art.

All she was capable of was experiencing the unique, paralysing pleasure of this man she'd thought she hated, but had somehow agreed to marry. The man who had been front and centre of her most sexually charged dreams for many years.

They'd said that this was just sex, and it was. It had to be. But in the back of her mind, she knew that nothing with them could ever truly be that simple. Not because of their baby, but because of something else. Something more. From the first moment they'd met, there'd been an undercurrent of understanding. Even when they'd hardly known each other she'd *felt* that she did know him.

But there was no way she intended to dwell on those thoughts. Even if Rosie had been interested in an actual relationship—and she wasn't—Aristotle would be the worst candidate on the face of the earth. Not least because he clearly had no interest in getting involved with anyone.

His body was collapsed on top of hers, their breathing ragged, dragged from them as though they'd run a marathon. Sweat sheened her skin and her hands ran distractedly down his back, on either side of his spine, as the fog of sensual satisfaction thickened and clung to her, sweet and addictive.

He pushed up onto one elbow and she instantly missed his body weight. His warmth. The feeling of his heart thumping against her.

His eyes met hers, then scanned her face, falling to her lips and hovering there, as his own quirked downwards, into a contemplative frown. His hand moved towards her brow, sweeping her hair back, then stayed just at her temple, fingers curled towards his palm.

'You are beautiful.' His voice had that same accented rawness she'd noticed earlier. Usually, he spoke English almost like a native, but right now, spent from what they'd just done, he was different.

She studied him, her heart jolting in her chest at the sight of him like that. Ever since she'd known him, she'd thought of him as wild and elemental. A man who seemed to exist half in this world and half in another, like some mythical creature.

But *here*, like this?

He was sheer, untamed, uncivilized man beast. And if she wasn't very careful, she could get addicted to this—and him. Far from getting him out of her system, it would be so easy to crave this regularly.

Which she couldn't allow to happen.

'That was...great,' she said, pleased her voice only sounded a little tremulous. She pressed a hand to his chest, forcing herself to dig deep, to reinforce everything they'd agreed before. To cling to it like a lifeline, because that resolve *would* save her. It would keep this neat, just like they both wanted.

But his hand at her temple moved to her lips, stroking her there, before coming to rest on the mattress beside her.

'Yes.' Simple, but effective. Her heart rammed harder into her ribs. 'You look worried.'

She blinked, surprised. 'Do I?'

'Are you?'

She stared at him, contemplated obfuscating. But they both needed to remember the boundaries. After what they'd just shared, it felt even more important to recommit to what they'd agreed.

'I just want to be clear about what just happened,' she said carefully. 'I'm not someone who has casual sex with guys, so I don't know how this is meant to work. But the whole reason we're getting married is to give our baby everything we want for them. I know that's not some messy, complicated situation. So...we need to be clear, and careful.'

His features were almost mocking. 'Do you think I'm going to fall in love with you, Rosemary?'

Heat flushed her cheeks and she flicked her eyes heavenward. 'I don't think you're capable of it,' she quipped, not realising until that moment that she did, in fact, think that of him.

And the thought left her with a heaviness in her belly that she couldn't seem to dispel.

'You're right,' he said after a beat, his face carefully blanked of any emotion. 'So there's no risk here.'

Her lips pulled to the side. 'Why are you like this?'

'I could ask you the same question.'

'You already know.'

'So you're going to be single forever because your parents' marriage was a shitshow?'

She stared at him, frowning. 'I'm marrying you,' she pointed out.

'For the sake of our baby. It's not a death sentence.'

Her heart lurched. Stupidly, she hadn't even thought about the duration of their marriage. She'd actually let the whole 'till death do us part' thing lodge in her brain and stay there.

'What does that mean?'

He pushed up from her fully then, stretching to stand and looking down at her body as though needing one final sight, before he turned away and reached for his boxer briefs, pulling them on with that powerful athleticism that was innate to him.

'It's in the contract.'

She blinked at him.

'A thousand years ago, or so it seems, I came in to get you to sign this.'

He looked around then reached to the ground, lifting up a stapled collection of white paper.

'Prenuptial agreement?'

'That's part of it,' he agreed. 'Let's go through it over dinner.'

They'd just shared an act of incredible intimacy, but with him now partially dressed and looking down at her as he resumed a calm, businesslike tone, she felt self-conscious all of a sudden. She moved then, scrambling out of the bed and looking around for her own clothes. They were spread too far. She unhooked the robe from the back of her door instead and wrapped it around her body, cinching it gently at the waist then letting her hand hover there, over their baby.

When she turned to face him, he was staring at her. At her stomach. A look on his features that took her breath away because it was so rich with emotion.

'I still can't believe it's happening,' he said, voice difficult to analyse. Deep and husky, rich with the same feelings that were stamped on his features.

She dropped her hand to the side. 'It does seem… far-fetched.'

'Improbable,' he agreed with a nod.

'I was on the pill, you know,' she said. 'I took it religiously. I never planned…'

A frown flickered across his face. 'I didn't think for one minute that you had.'

'It's just… I know some women might think this—and you—are the epitome of their dreams.' She bit into her lip, thinking of her archaeological sites and the certainty she'd once had that those were where she belonged. For the first time in her life, she'd felt wanted and valued.

'But you're not one of them.'

'It's not you, per se—'

'Ahh, it's not you, it's me.'

She smiled at that. 'It's my work.'

His eyes narrowed. 'Let's have dinner—you'll see there is a section in here that deals with that.'

The contracts were beyond thorough. Not only was there a section dealing with her work, and how they'd manage her travel needs with a baby—a combination of a nanny, his private jet and the understanding that she would avoid sites that held unacceptable risks to herself or the child—there seemed to be a section on pretty much everything.

'This thing covers what happens if I die, you die, we divorce, we separate, we fight but don't leave each other, where we choose to live, to send our child to school, make medical decisions, grandparent visitations, Christmas traditions. You've really thought of everything,' she said.

He sat back in his chair, dressed casually in a T-shirt and jeans. 'My legal team drafted it. Let's talk about changes.'

She flicked through the thick wodge of papers. At the back, there was a table of financial considerations, including an eye-watering trust fund he would set up for their child, as well as a stipend to be paid to Rosie. It made her skin crawl, in a way. She'd worked for a long time; supporting herself was a part of that. He'd implied in the past that her father might have married his mother for the money; she hated him to think that was a factor for her at all. And yet, what were her options? She could do home-based work for a while, earning an income to cover her basic needs. She had some savings on hand, though they were rapidly dwindling, thanks to her redecorating efforts.

'I don't want to rely on you,' she blurted out after a beat, eyes fixed on the financial table. 'I've worked since leaving school.'

He leaned forward then, his expression hawkish. 'You're about to have a baby.'

She nodded, brushing a hand over her stomach, heart twisting. ‘Lots of women still work.’

‘I have no issues with that. But your work is not exactly easy to accommodate with a child in tow. The provisions will make it manageable, though obviously we would need to limit the amount of time you are out of the country.’

She blinked at him.

‘We’re getting married so I can be in his or her life. I can see how important your job is to you—I would not walk away from my business interests, either. But I intend for my child to be raised with me.’

‘I never saw you as the paternal type, Aristotle.’

His eyes held hers for a beat. ‘That makes two of us.’

But he was brushing her off. Giving her a pithy response rather than explaining why he’d reacted so strongly. Something though had locked into place inside of her, telling her that, without a shadow of a doubt, there was a reason for him to have reacted as he had. In London, he’d virtually kidnapped her, and left no real possibility for her to refuse his proposal.

‘You know what’s not in here?’

He waited for her to continue, but there was a wariness to him now, as though he knew questions had been raised inside of her that she wanted answered.

‘The day-to-day stuff.’

‘Such as?’

‘What time will you be home from work? Will we eat dinner together as a family, like this?’ She gestured to the table. ‘Will you help with bathtime? Read books to the child after dinner? Will you take him or her to school, or does that fall to a nanny—or me? How often do we go home to your mother’s, to see our parents? What about my mother in London?’

He sat back in his chair, his face a study in relaxation. 'Some things will have to work out as we go.'

'But what kind of father will you be? You keep saying you want to be here for our child. What does that mean?'

'I want to be in their life.'

'In what way?'

'Isn't it obvious?'

'This is the first time I've seen you pretty much since we got to Athens,' she pointed out. 'You leave for work early, you come home late. Is that what it will be like when they're born? Will "being there" for our child mean kisses on their forehead while they sleep?'

'No,' he denied flatly and then, with another quick show of emotion, he reached for his water glass, hand curling around it until his knuckles were white. 'It means I'll be in their life, however they need.'

She contemplated that. 'This contract is the most thorough document I've ever read. You have a paragraph in here about what happens if either of us ends up in a coma, for God's sake. I don't think it's unreasonable to discuss the far more likely future outcomes.'

'I have no opinion on this,' he said after a beat, placing the glass down slightly harder than necessary.

'You are a man who has an opinion on everything.'

'Not children, and how to raise them.'

'Yet you're adamant that getting married is the "only" way. Why?'

His eyes narrowed. 'Are you regretting your acceptance of my proposal?'

'It wasn't a proposal, and we both know it. It was an insistence.'

A muscle jerked low in his jaw. 'What would you have done if our positions had been reversed?'

'And you were pregnant with my baby?'

It was a joke, but it fell flat. His expression didn't change. His eyes continued to bore into her with a look of barely contained frustration.

'If I somehow had the power to make all the parenting decisions, and chose to keep you out of their life. If you had the ability to act, to pull whatever strings you could to make sure that wouldn't happen, wouldn't you have done it?'

She opened her mouth to say something, but his words replayed in her head, and a different kind of comprehension dawned, suspicion unfolding. 'Is that why you slept with me just now?' she asked. His expression shifted then, but she didn't notice. 'Was it some kind of insurance policy? A way to keep me here, in case I don't sign this?'

He stared at her as though she'd sprouted ten heads. 'If I had my way, our marriage would be this—' he gestured to the contract '—and nothing more. Sex should be no part of this.'

'Just what every woman likes to hear.'

'You are *not* every woman, Rosemary. You are pregnant with my child, and soon you will be my wife. Our marriage will run more smoothly if we don't make that mistake again.'

She winced at that.

'You know it was a mistake,' he growled, but he moved then, reaching out and putting his hand over hers, so sparks began to simmer just beneath her skin. 'But it was the most enjoyable mistake I've ever made. Including the other two times we've slept together. I should never have been with you. Not once. Not twice. Not tonight. But there is something about you…'

Her throat felt thick as she swallowed. 'It won't happen again,' she said, pulling her hand away and caressing it in her lap. The sparks he'd ignited were like flames now. 'You know, I'm really tired. All that dangerous scaling of ladders, you know…'

'That reminds me,' he said, not missing a beat. 'I'm putting in a handyman clause.'

She was too emotionally drained to argue with him. 'Do what you want,' she said, pushing back her chair. 'I'll see you tomorrow,' she said, with no idea if that was true or not.

The last thought Aristotle had before giving up on sleep altogether was the realisation that sleeping with Rosemary definitely hadn't succeeded in getting her out of his system. If anything, it had driven her deep, deep inside of it, so she was all he could think of, all he could want.

He'd thought that going over the contract with a simple platter dinner would re-establish a businesslike footing, putting them both on the same page once more. Removing sex from the equation. But watching Rosemary eat was its own torturous kind of foreplay. The way her fingers delicately collected grapes and popped them into her mouth, her lips juicy from the olives, her cheeks still flushed from being made love to, her hair tousled in a way that made him itch to reach over and grab it, to drag her head to his so he could kiss her senseless for the rest of the night.

Having sex with Rosemary had been a mistake, just like he'd said, but, unlike most mistakes Aristotle had ever made, this was one he couldn't promise he wouldn't repeat. Even when he knew he shouldn't, every fibre of his being was aching to be with her again. So much so he wanted to forget about common sense and go to her room and kiss her awake, stir her to that same fever-pitch she'd been in for him earlier that evening.

Of course, he'd never do it. He was on the brink of losing control, but he still had just enough left to keep those feelings at bay.

He gave up on sleep though, and stalked into the bathroom instead, turning the tap to blast icy water out. A cold shower might help—at least, for now.

CHAPTER TEN

'GOOD MORNING. COFFEE?'

She startled as, bleary-eyed, she entered the kitchen to find Aristotle very much still *in situ*. Her hands instinctively reached for the short hem of her nightshirt—it barely covered her hips. Then again, she'd had no expectation of finding him here. Based on past experience, Aristotle was usually gone by now.

Today, though, he wasn't even wearing a suit.

'Why aren't you at work?' she asked defensively, thinking of the bird's nest that was her hair and her make-up-free face. She glanced quickly at the clock which showed it was after eight.

When she looked back at him, her pulse went into overdrive, because his gaze was roaming her body as though mentally undressing her, remembering every curve and indent of skin, every colour and shade, every inch.

'Aristotle—' she said unevenly.

It was meant to be a warning, but she heard the longing in her voice. The plea. *Take me.* She swallowed quickly. Last night *had* been a mistake, but as for getting him out of her system, there wasn't a hope in hell of it being so quickly achieved.

'We didn't finish our negotiation last night.'

'Is that what that was?'

'Every contract is a starting point. This is a draft. I expect you to have changes to make.'

'And you'll go along with them?'

'If they're reasonable. Hence the term *negotiation*.'

Her eyes fell to the document between them as his words took on a whole new meaning. Or perhaps it was that they coincided with the thoughts she was already having, about the way they sparked off each other, and how hard it would be to contain that.

'I think we should write in a sex clause,' she said, half holding her breath.

The air between them thickened and sparked with electricity.

'As in, no sex?' His voice was hard to read.

She moved to the contract and flicked through the corners, fidgeting her way through the awkwardness of this. 'I don't think that's practical.'

More sparks in the atmosphere, and she felt her skin tingling.

'We have to make sure it is.'

'But what if there's another way?' she insisted.

'Okay. I'll humour you.'

Her lip twisted at that. Last night, over dinner, it had been easy to let those old doubts creep back in, her lack of confidence with men, and this man in particular, ingrained in Rosie. But she wasn't that shy twenty-year-old any more, and she had no reason to doubt that Aristotle's desire for her was authentic. And as overpowering as her own for him.

'Do you want me?' she asked, crossing her arms over her chest, ignoring the intense vulnerability that came from asking this question.

He stared at her for so long that the vulnerability stretched and grew, but then he nodded once. ‘Obviously.’

A spark of pleasure ignited in her bloodstream. His honesty was not a surprise, but it was very welcome.

‘Did last night make you want me less?’

She held her breath, waiting for his answer, hoping it would match hers.

‘Aristotle?’ she prompted when he just stared at her wordlessly for so long she wondered if he was going to ignore her.

‘No.’ The word almost seemed dragged from him, from the depths of his soul, against his will. ‘If anything, the opposite is true.’

Triumph flared inside of her. ‘I feel the same,’ she said quickly. ‘Honestly, I think we’d be naïve to stand here and act like it’s not going to happen again.’

His jaw clenched. ‘We do have a say in that.’

‘Do we?’ she murmured. ‘If that were true, last night would never have happened, right?’

He dragged a hand through his hair and shifted his head in what she took to be a nod.

‘So, what if we prepare for that?’

He crossed his arms, studying her, waiting for her to continue.

She glanced down at the contract, flicking the corners once more. ‘Let’s try to build in some parameters around it. Such as how often is okay, and the fact we both know it’s just a physical thing. Like an itch we have to scratch from time to time. Until we don’t.’

‘Until we’re over it?’ he prompted.

She nodded quickly. ‘And how that happens. I just think it’s super unrealistic to pretend we can control this.’ She swallowed. ‘I mean, maybe it’s hormones, or the fact we made a baby together, but it’s just hard to imagine us living together and *not* occasionally making that same mistake all over again.'

He continued to stare at her.

'So, given that this contract covers pretty much every contingency imaginable, it would be shortsighted not to include a sex clause.'

'Just in case.'

She nodded once.

'Agreed.'

She let out a breath she hadn't realised she'd been holding onto. 'I mean, we don't have to get your lawyers to actually put it into the contract. We can do it ourselves.' She flushed to the roots of her hair. 'The contract, I mean.'

His eyes sparked to hers, amusement lighting their obsidian depths. He reached for the front page of the contract, which had only their names on it, and turned it over, then retrieved a pen from the top drawer.

> *On the occasions that Aristotle Machairas and Rosemary Machairas/Richardson have sex, both parties acknowledge it means nothing.*

She read along over his shoulder, and suggested, 'Both parties agree to notify the other if they develop feelings.'

He transcribed that, word for word.

'Anything else?' she murmured, only now realising how close she was standing to him, and taking a subtle step to the side.

He began to write once more.

> *If either party wishes to initiate a sexual relationship with another person, they will first discuss it with the parties to this agreement.*

Her heart pounded hard then dropped to her toes. She hadn't even thought about other people. With good reason. It wasn't as though she'd had a hectic dating life. Between the two times she'd had ill-considered sex with the man she was going to marry, she'd been with two other men. Both short-lived, unsatisfying and uncomplicated. But Aristotle was nothing like Rosie. He'd been with more women than he could count.

'Good?' he asked, turning to face her, with no idea of the small emotional bomb that was detonating inside of her. The parts of her that wanted to scream *nooooo* at the thought of Artistotle—her husband-to-be, the father of her child—having affairs with other women. Oh, he'd no doubt be very discreet, for the sake of their child, and his reputation, but what did that matter?

She'd be married to him, knowing he was driving other women wild, while she was home with their baby?

Her stomach twisted at the perils of the situation she found herself in. She couldn't say why it unsettled her so much, because emotions weren't involved. Yet a possessive heat stole through her, making it impossible to contemplate a time when this man would not be hers. She stifled the thought immediately.

He was not hers.

He'd probably never be anyone's.

And that was for the best, because Rosie felt exactly the same way.

She'd seen first-hand what that kind of possessiveness could do to a person, and a life. Her mother had 'loved' her father to the point of derangement. When he'd chosen to leave she'd sought out every tool at her disposal to make his life miserable. To destroy him however she could, including withholding his only daughter from him.

That sort of attachment—'love'—was a recipe for disaster.

It was completely outside of what Rosie ever wanted in her life.

'Good,' she agreed, forcing a breezy-seeming smile as her eyes dropped back to the contract. 'Perfect. Shall we shake on it?'

He turned to face her, and the sparks that were humming just beneath the surface exploded in a multicolour array of lights and heat. 'I can think of better ways.'

She pushed up onto the tips of her toes, face angled to his. 'Such as?'

He wrapped his arms around her back, pulling her to him and lifting her onto the kitchen bench, so he stood between her legs, kissing her masterfully, until there were no thoughts of other women, of contracts, of anything but this in her mind, and it was a state of bliss—even when she knew it was temporary.

Aristotle had always favoured 'no commitment' relationships. No promises. Nothing serious. He had shied away from any sort of commitment, from anything that he might come to depend on—and then risk losing. At first, it hadn't been a conscious decision. He'd just ended things whenever his partner had seemed too serious, breaking up with a woman before she could break up with him. At some point, he'd realised what he was doing, and why.

He didn't need a masters in psychology to recognise that everything could be traced back to the discovery of his adoption. The sense that his whole self-view had been forged on a lie. Nothing and no one could be trusted. It was a protective shield, in the same way this contract was.

Because with Rosemary, and their baby, he was doing

something he'd never, ever wanted. He was opening himself up to someone else. Not Rosemary per se, but their baby. In committing to be in this baby's life, he was committing to be a parent, a father.

For all that his own father had kept the truth of his parentage from him, he had also been an excellent role model. A steady constant in Aristotle's life, until he wasn't.

But in order to enter into this marriage, his 'family', he needed some protections. Some guarantees that there were guardrails in place to prevent it from getting messy. To protect him from wanting more from Rosemary than was wise—to protect them both.

The sex clause was a chef's kiss inclusion, because she was absolutely right. As was evidenced by how they'd just spent the past hour, slavishly worshipping each other's bodies until they were both utterly satiated. There was no way they could live in the same space, share meals, glances, accidental touches, and not have the pressure between them build to breaking point. Again and again. He didn't know when it would burn out—surely at some point—but having a clearly defined agreement about what they were doing, and how they'd manage it, was yet another guardrail he needed.

And in spelling everything out so clearly—in writing, and with Rosemary at his side, in lockstep with him—he felt as though a weight had been lifted off him that he hadn't even known he'd carried. The pressure of always working to keep people at arm's length evaporated completely. He didn't need to work so hard, because they had a contract.

Rosemary was someone who wanted an emotional entanglement even less than he did.

Aristotle smiled as he pressed another coffee through the machine, mentally tabulating the list of things they needed to do today. Planning to spend time with Rosemary without even a hint of concern. Usually, he would use his work as a barrier. The long hours he spent at his desk were, if nothing else, a way to maintain strict personal boundaries. He didn't need that now, *vis-à-vis* the contract, and her willingness to go along with it.

Which left him free to let go and just enjoy…

It didn't occur to him to worry at that point just *how much* he was enjoying the thought of spending the day with Rosemary. And why, if he was smart, he would run a mile, before it was too late.

'What do you think?'

The midday sun was warm on her skin, and Rosemary tilted her face upwards to enjoy it for a moment. Between that and the way Aristotle had his hand protectively in the small of her back, holding her close to his side, and the husky note in his accented voice, Rosemary had the sense that everything was just as it should be. For real this time. Not pretend. Not make-believe.

The contract negotiations had actually turned the whole fake marriage idea into something real for her. It wasn't what most people thought of when they dreamed of marriage, but that didn't mean it wouldn't work for them. In fact, the neat, clinical terms of the relationship were probably the only way either of them would ever enter into any kind of relationship.

Somehow, they'd taken the bomb detonation of her pregnancy and found a way to make it work.

'Rosemary?'

He always put the emphasis on the first part of the first syllable, his tongue landing heavily on the R. It was her favourite way to hear her name now. She tilted her face slightly, away from the sun's warmth and towards his instead.

'Of what?'

His lips flickered into a small smile, but his eyes quickly creased with concern. 'You sound tired. Would you rather go home?'

'That depends,' she said, slowing to a stop. 'How many more of these have you arranged?'

'One more,' he said, then pulled a face. 'Too much?'

They'd spent the entire morning interviewing obstetricians and touring hospitals. Not just from Greece. Oh, no. Aristotle Machairas had flown top obstetricians in from across Europe, and one from the UAE.

'No,' she said. 'I mean yes, it is, actually.' She laughed then, pressing a hand to his chest and revelling in the freedom to do that. To touch when she wanted to touch. Because it wasn't a loaded promise; it didn't mean anything. It was just a physical act, like sex. Nothing intimate or real about it. 'I really do want minimal medical interventions, Aristotle. That last doctor spent the entire time going through emergency delivery procedures. I have no doubt she can cope *if* that happens, but I really want to focus on the fact I'm young, healthy and everything looked fine in the scan we had last week.'

'Of course. But it's a good idea to have a backup plan.'

'Yeah,' she admitted, nibbling on her lower lip, not wanting to point out that any obstetrician in any of these hospitals would undoubtedly be qualified. There was no point. When it came to their baby, Aristotle Machairas had made it clear: he would take no risks, and no expense would be spared.

'I can do the appointment alone,' he offered. 'The driver can take you on to lunch. Or home, if you'd prefer to put your feet up.'

'Lunch?' She instantly perked up at the idea of food.

He grinned, his whole face changing into a mask of pleasure and amusement. Her heart scampered.

'I've booked a place I think you'll like.'

The next obstetrician was, for Rosie, a clear winner. She was experienced, confident, funny and reassuring, and one of the first things she remarked on, having viewed the ultrasound images, was the likelihood that Rosie's pregnancy and delivery should be straightforward. She concurred with Rosie's hopes for a medically non-invasive pregnancy if possible, and essentially made Rosie feel as if she was doing everything right.

Her mood was already elevated, therefore, when they left the obstetrician's office, but it lifted even further as Aristotle took her to the elevator and pressed the up button rather than down. On the roof, there was a sleek white helicopter with tinted windows that he guided her to. She could only glance at him with brows raised as one of the two security guards in dark suits opened the rear door for them to settle into the plush leather seats, separated from the pilot by a dark screen.

'Is this yours?' she asked as Aristotle handed over a set of headsets with a short nod. She slid them on, but a moment later Aristotle was reaching across and pressing a button on the side. They immediately dimmed the outside noise, and when Aristotle next spoke, she heard him as clearly as if he was talking right into her ear.

'Seatbelt,' he said, gesturing to the sash to her left. She fastened it in place as the rotor blades began to spin and then they were lifting up, over Athens, so she craned her neck to look out of the window, staring at the incredible city—a patchwork of white stone buildings and terracotta rooftops, with the Acropolis glistening white on this flawlessly sun-soaked day.

A contented sigh escaped her lips as her eyes roamed the city. 'Did you know it used to be brightly coloured?' she asked, pointing towards the Acropolis.

'Yes.'

'Of course you do.' She flashed him an apologetic smile. 'You grew up here. There's probably nothing about this city you don't know.'

'I'm sure that's not true. But my father was into history—'

'I remember.' Another smile, softer this time. Sympathetic.

'He liked to talk to me about it. He was very proud of his heritage.'

She reached out and put her hand on his thigh and squeezed, again thinking how grateful she was to be able to do that now. It was so simple, except it wasn't, because there was a burst of awareness that flared in her belly at even that simple touch. Still, she kept her hand there instead of withdrawing it quickly, because his voice had taken on a rawness that pulled at something in her belly. She knew his father had meant a lot to him, but the emotion in his voice surprised her.

'Where are we going?' she asked, glancing back towards the window as the helicopter floated towards the sparkling Aegean, leaving the city in the distance.

'You'll see.'

She glanced at him. 'A surprise?'

'Isn't that the theme of our relationship?' he asked, but his lips flickered in a smile and she smiled back, putting the somersaulting in her stomach down to the helicopter's speed.

CHAPTER ELEVEN

From the moment the helicopter touched down on the small mountainous island she knew she was in for something special. The helipad was in a clearing a mile or so in from the coastline and a sleek black SUV was waiting for them upon landing. Aristotle kept a hand around Rosie, on her hip, as they disembarked and then walked, so she was tucked close to his side.

They were driven along a narrow road, through the forest, and then they began to wind their way up a steep mountain, the track clinging to the side, so for much of the time they had a spectacular view of the island, the water and the mainland in the distance.

'Where exactly are we?'

'Tharkos.'

She turned to face him then. 'There are supposed to be some incredible Minoan ruins here, you know.'

'Are there?' he responded, but in a tone that told her he did indeed know. Not only that, he'd brought her here specifically.

As the car approached the top of the mountain, she remembered reading about a world-famous, impossible-to-get-into restaurant that had opened up on the island, catering to the very well-heeled tourist trade. The thought literally came to her at the same time the restaurant came into view, and her heart skipped a beat. Both with excitement at being here and at the fact he'd organised it.

'Aristotle—' she said, shaking her head a little, but not finishing the sentence because emotions were suddenly flooding her, making it hard to speak without crying.

'I thought you'd like it,' he said simply.

She nodded once as the driver came to open the car door. She stepped out, glancing down at her casual summer dress with a grimace.

'You look beautiful,' Aristotle said, unnerving her a little with how easily he could interpret her thoughts. Then he was lacing his fingers through hers and tugging her gently towards the large glass doors of the restaurant.

The restaurant itself was a spectacular design. The walls were almost completely made of glass, to showcase the views, on three sides the ocean and on the fourth the mountain, covered in trees and being roamed, to Rosie's delight, by goats. The roof was skillion style, so the side of the building overlooking Athens had a particularly high window, and the furnishings were sleek and modern. But it was the ruins the building was designed to maximise that had her heart turning over in her chest. The floor itself was tiled, but in various places, thick glass had been used to show what was beneath—carefully excavated and studied Minoan ruins, including amazingly coloured frescoes that set her pulse firing.

'It's wonderful,' she murmured as they were seated at a table by the glass. Despite the open-plan nature of the venue and the minimalism of the furnishings, indoor plants were used with great effect, to both soften the harshness of the interior and create small private areas. Their table was mostly shielded from the others, and she was glad.

'Did you ever come here with your dad?' she asked. She

was genuinely curious, but also, she was sure there'd been something in his tone in the helicopter, when he'd mentioned his father's heritage.

'No.' There it was again. A tightening. A pushing away.

Curiosity deepened.

'Was it built before he passed away?'

'I believe it's been here around ten years.'

'Interesting that he never brought you here, given his love of history.'

His jaw clenched visibly. 'We weren't that close.'

She frowned. That was true.

'You were away a lot,' she said carefully, approaching this from a different angle.

He nodded once, and when a waiter passed, Aristotle lifted his hand to call him over. They'd only been seated a minute or so. It was pretty clear he was looking for a distraction, to end the conversation. Which only made her more determined. She waited as he ordered some water and bread, then, before he could start a new topic, she pushed on.

'Were you always…not close with them?'

A muscle jerked in his jaw. He looked around, but there was no one else to rescue him.

'It's complicated.'

'What does that mean?'

He expelled a harsh breath before turning back to her, his eyes landing on hers. His lips twisted downwards, as though he was lost in thought. She held her breath, waiting to see if he'd speak or not, with a sixth sense telling her that this was important.

'When I was fifteen, I discovered I was adopted.'

Rosie sat up straighter, every cell in her body tensing with alertness. 'I'm sorry—did you say *adopted*?'

His smile lacked humour. It was a ghastly stretching of

his lips. 'You said it yourself: I don't look anything like my parents.'

'You don't,' she admitted, shaking her head. 'But you're so like your father. In mannerisms and determination, even the sound of your voice…'

'I was adopted,' he said slowly, carefully. 'I can only presume those are learned traits. That having been raised by him, I picked some of it up. I have no earthly idea who my biological parents are, nor why they gave me away.'

Though the building was clearly impeccably crafted, she felt almost as though she'd been caught in a landslide and was slipping down towards the ocean in a cascade of rubble and grief. *'Why they gave me away.'* It was such a simple statement, but she heard the hurt behind it, the pain.

'Did your parents know?'

His eyes hooked to hers. 'What do you mean?'

'Did they know anything about your biological parents?'

He frowned. 'Not that I am aware of.'

'You've asked them?'

He shifted in his seat, eyes moving back to the view. 'My mother has no idea I know the truth.'

She gasped. 'What?'

He turned back to her, his eyes awash with emotion. 'When I found out, I confronted my father about it. He confirmed that I was adopted, told me it didn't matter, and that I was never to bring it up with my mother. That was the end of it. He refused to discuss it further.'

Anger fired in Rosie's veins. 'That was incredibly selfish of him,' she said. 'This is *your* life. You have a right to know these things, if you want to.'

He dipped his head down once. 'There was no sense pursuing it. He was adamant that the information was "closed", the file that might provide answers non-existent. There was no sense in upsetting my mother when it wouldn't give me the information I sought. So I let it go.'

She shook her head once, but before she could speak, the waiter returned with water and bread.

'Would you like to order anything else?'

Frustrated by the interruption, Rosie turned to him and said, 'Just bring us whatever the chef recommends. Oh, that's safe for someone pregnant.'

The waiter smiled broadly. 'Congratulations, madam, sir. Of course. Please, enjoy.' He gestured to the bread and then, to her relief, departed swiftly.

She leaned forward, covering Aristotle's hand with her own. 'But you didn't let it go, did you?'

He glanced at her, expression inscrutable.

'You stopped coming home. You stewed on this; you fumed about it. And you've been reserved with your parents ever since.'

He reached for his drink with his spare hand and took a long gulp. 'Do you blame me?'

'No, I blame them,' she said swiftly. 'Your father should have supported you through this more. Finding out that you're adopted must have shaken you to the core.'

He nodded once, his eyes sparking with something like appreciation. 'It was as though the foundations of my whole life—my entire being—crumbled beneath me. I had no idea who I was any more.'

'Of course,' she said.

'I looked in the mirror and saw a stranger. I lived with my parents yet no longer had a sense of belonging. I accept now what my father said: they chose to love me, to raise me as their own. In every way that matters, I am their son. But there is a huge part of me filled with unanswered questions. I hate that.'

'I'm so sorry,' she said with heartfelt sympathy. 'Is this why you were so adamant that our baby would know you?'

'Would know that they are wanted,' he corrected slightly. 'I never wanted children,' he admitted. 'But from the moment I learned of your pregnancy, *this*—' he gestured from himself to her '—has felt like the only option. The right thing.'

'Yes,' she admitted. She'd agreed with him almost the entire time, anyway. Not that two people who made a baby needed to get married. It was the twenty-first century and in fact she thought generally it was a terrible reason for marriage. But for Aristotle and her, and given everything they'd each been through, it was the only option.

'Are you telling me your mother has no idea you know about being adopted?'

He nodded once.

'I really think you should have this conversation with her.'

'My father prohibited it.'

'That was a long time ago.'

'Perhaps if he was alive, I would bring it up again now. But I cannot disregard his request. It was very important to him that my mother be protected from the pain of this discussion.'

Rosie's temper flared. 'And what about you? Who was protecting you?'

His lips pulled to the side. 'I've done a good enough job of protecting myself,' he pointed out, and Rosie's heart sank. Because, just like that, all of the pieces of the puzzle that was Aristotle whooshed together—fragments that suddenly formed a perfect image of the man across from her. The way the discovery of his adoption had damaged him, so that he pushed everyone away, determined never to rely on someone again, to seek the sort of family and comfort he'd once known.

His whole lifestyle of ruthless independence was not predicated on anything other than having once been a devastated, hurt fifteen-year-old. Over a decade later, he still carried those wounds, and if he wasn't careful, they'd ruin his life.

And what about you? You're one to talk, that snide little voice jeered. Because she had also let her childhood wounds dictate her adult choices. Just like Aristotle, she'd taken the hurt of being used as a pawn, to wound her father, knowing her mother didn't see her as anything other than a weapon. Knowing that as soon as her mother had remarried and had more children, Rosie had become completely dispensable.

How could she trust, let alone love, when her example of maternal love was so flawed?

She looked across at Aristotle and the sinking of her heart turned into something else entirely. More puzzle pieces began to slide together. This time, they were not pieces of him, but rather, of them.

The sense she'd felt, even at fourteen, that on the day they'd met, he was somehow a part of her. She'd felt it every time they'd seen each other afterwards, too. When their eyes would meet. In the thickening of the air around them, the stampeding of her heart.

She'd put it down to a childish girlhood crush, that she'd outgrown. And then, to sexual chemistry. And now? Their shared need to do what was right for their child.

But what if something else was at play? Something more.

She frowned across at him as a deeper understanding of her feelings began to take hold, even when she didn't want it to. She tried to stop the thoughts in their tracks, to push aside her shifting perception of this situation. Because she *couldn't* fall in love with Aristotle Machairas. She refused to love anyone, having seen the destructive effects up close.

The joke, of course—and it was not a particularly funny one—was that Rosie had believed, all her life, that she could control her heart. That wishing it to not be vulnerable to love meant it wouldn't be.

How stupid she'd been.

How incredibly naïve.

She was an archaeologist and, no matter where she went and which culture she was studying, she had often reflected on the commonalities of all cultures and communities across time. The emotional similarities—valour, jealousy, grief and love. These were uniform and observable in all societies, regardless of the variations in tribalism, trappings, religious observances.

How had she thought she could exempt herself from any of those key human conditions?

It wasn't that her heart was immune to love, as she'd so long supposed, but rather it had been lost, without her realising it. Lost to Aristotle, and from that moment on, no one else had been able to get a look in. She'd been able to stay single without giving it a second thought because all of her heart, her mind and soul were already spoken for.

Her lips parted on a rush of breath as the realisations continued to detonate in her brain, one after the other.

He turned his hand over and captured hers, squeezing it. 'Rosemary, is something wrong? You look as though you've seen a ghost.'

She blinked quickly, her heart twisting. Her heart. Her stupid, disloyal heart! How on earth could it have been so stupid? To fall for Aristotle, the first time she'd met him? For as sure as she now knew that she loved him, she knew that this was a path destined to lead to devastation.

It was impossible to imagine he would ever love her back.

For while her hurts were historical, his were ongoing. His uncertainty about his parentage, the gap in his knowledge, was a wound that continued to bruise him daily.

'When this baby is born,' she murmured, curving her hand over her stomach as she glanced across at him, 'how will you cope with the fact that you might look into their face and see features you don't recognise? A throwback to your biological parents, perhaps, or someone else?'

His jaw tightened. 'I don't know.'

Her chest felt as though something heavy was being pushed into it.

'It is one of the reasons I never wanted to have children. To look down into their face and not know it, to not be able to answer that child's questions about our history, our family's past… I have no idea what genetic burden I am passing on, what traits.'

Tears filled her eyes, as the whole future she'd imagined somehow seemed impossible to navigate now.

'You have to talk to your mother,' she said, knowing that was the only course of action that could give them hope. 'You have to ask if she knows anything.'

'She doesn't.'

'Your father said that, but maybe she does. Maybe things have changed now. Either way, she should know that you know the truth.'

He jerked his gaze towards the ocean. 'I didn't tell you as a means to ask for advice. I've known this for years, and that knowledge is a part of me.'

'So is the hurt and doubt,' she said firmly. 'You're living with a bruise you might not need to carry.'

'Do you think there is anything my mother could say that would change that?'

'I think you'll never have a proper relationship with her unless you're honest about this. I think you both deserve better than that.'

He turned to face her, eyes spearing her with their intensity. 'I told you because it's an important part of who I am—something you should understand, as we embark on this life together. It changes nothing about me, our marriage, and how I feel about our child. Please do not give it another moment's thought, and for God's sake, don't mention it to her—or anyone.'

He didn't regret telling her. They were going to be parents; it felt appropriate for her to understand the unknowability of his DNA.

He just regretted the *way* in which he'd told her. Even as the words had spilled out, he'd heard the defensiveness in his tone. Even when he'd known she was trying to look at the problem and find a solution, to offer a fresh perspective, he'd just wanted to shut it down.

She couldn't possibly understand what discovering his adoption had done to him.

So too his father's refusal to help him find the answers he needed. In fact, his father had flat-out refused to have another conversation about it. He'd clearly expected Aristotle to be able to compartmentalize this part of his life, to bury it and move on.

But he never had.

Even now, it was so easy to feel like that fifteen-year-old again. And Rosemary had only amplified that, with her soft sympathy and gentle urging to talk to his mother.

He wanted to remind her that he was a monolith, a man who lived his own life unaffected by anyone else, untouched by need or wants, but the words hadn't come.

For all that his independence was his identity, it was no longer accurate to describe him as that alone. Their baby made it impossible—and so did Rosemary. She was a part of his life now, and always would be. She was the mother of his child, and no matter what happened, no matter where life and fate took him, caring for her, ensuring her well-being, would always be important.

Which was why he'd moved the conversation on, keeping the tone light, asking her questions about the Minoan culture, then about Athens, then about her more interesting digs, until she'd seemed, finally, to have given up on the subject of his adoption.

As they flew back over Athens and landed on the helipad atop his penthouse apartment, he knew she was different though. Deep in thought.

Which was the last thing he wanted. The subject of his adoption was something he'd sat with a long time. He refused to let it bleed into the present, to change the very successful arrangement he'd formed with Rosemary. And so, when they returned home, he did the one thing he could think of, and took her to bed, where nothing but their chemistry and connection seemed to matter.

CHAPTER TWELVE

She stirred early the next morning in a strange environment. Aristotle's room, with its impersonal monochromatic colour scheme—all shades of grey, cream and black—and modernistic furniture, and let her eyes shift over the room with renewed perception now.

She'd known he was cold.

Unattached.

But she'd thought that was his personality, rather than a byproduct of trauma. Now, she couldn't help but see the end result of his world-changing discovery on his entire life. In the lack of close friendships and relationships, in his one-eyed determination to succeed in business, as though he constantly had to prove himself. And finally, even in something as superficial as the décor of his penthouse.

The blandness didn't bother her because it was boring—although there was that. But it was the lack of *him* in the space, the lack of personal details, the cold, sterile furniture that had no history or connection to him. Despite the fact that his childhood home was overflowing with family heirlooms and sentimental items, he had brought none of them here with him. Not the candlesticks that were used as centrepieces each night for dinner, that had borne witness to presumably every shared family meal of his life. Not the artworks that hung on the walls, no family portraits, no chairs nor cushions that might remind him of life at the mansion on the hill.

It was austere in a way that was needless and now understandable. She turned to face him, at the exact moment his lashes fluttered and his eyes opened, latching to hers.

It was the first time they'd fallen asleep in the same bed; the first time they'd woken up side by side. But that wasn't what made her whole body bloom with warmth.

It was looking into his eyes with the knowledge she'd come to yesterday: that she loved him.

'Hi,' she said, the word emerging shy and soft, so she cleared her throat and flashed a smile at him, carefully obscuring any more complicated thoughts. 'How did you sleep?'

He reached out, tucking some hair behind her ear, his gaze resting on the auburn strands before slipping back to her eyes. 'Like a log. You?'

She stretched. 'Same.' She'd slept a dreamless sleep, and woken feeling more refreshed than she had in a long time.

'What time are you leaving for work today?'

He pushed up onto one elbow, regarding her thoughtfully. 'Actually, I thought I might take the day off.'

'You took yesterday off.'

'Which was my first leave day in about ten years,' he quipped. 'Unless you'd prefer to be left alone?'

Her heart jackhammered in her chest. 'That's not it,' she said quickly. 'I'm just…surprised.'

He reached up again, this time curving his hand over her cheek in a way that made her feel special and valued, vulnerable and reassured all at once. 'How else can I be sure you won't go scaling ladders?'

She laughed. 'You can't. You'd better book the next few

months off at least,' she suggested, ignoring the way her whole body tingled at the very idea. 'You know, in case I get any other decorating ideas.'

'Or set up my office from home,' he suggested, and she realised he wasn't even joking. 'It's probably a good idea to be around more. In case you need me.'

Her heart stammered.

'I can always go to the office for meetings—it's just a drive across town.'

'I'm fine, Aristotle,' she said, unevenly though, because knowing how she felt about him meant that this offer was setting her soul alight.

'I'd prefer not to leave anything to chance. This is our baby we're talking about,' he said, and the warmth ebbed slightly, leaving in its place a stark reminder that his actions were motivated by her pregnancy, rather than her. The fact that she loved Aristotle didn't mean he loved her. Or that he'd ever allow himself to.

The day before the wedding he woke up with a single compelling thought: every single part of their relationship made sense. It was like the best business partnerships he'd ever been in—where two people were in perfect harmony, their outlooks in sync. Everything about them just *worked.* Because of the contract? Or because of how compatible they were, in terms of forging a truly pragmatic relationship? It was as if they'd taken the standard model of a marriage and pulled out only the parts that suited them, to create something infinitely more workable, with zero chance of failure. How could things go wrong when their feelings weren't involved?

Okay, he wasn't completely naïve. Of course, some feelings were involved.

The walls they'd both kept up around themselves for various reasons had crumbled weeks ago, leaving in their place renewed understanding and respect. The woman who'd told him she hated him was no longer in evidence, and the man who'd had to threaten a legal battle to convince Rosemary of the wisdom of this marriage felt like a stranger. Because they understood one another so much better now, he couldn't conceive of a world in which he suggested marriage and she didn't immediately agree.

He woke with no hesitations or reservations about the next twenty-four hours. If anything, he simply felt a rush of adrenalin—and impatience—at the prospect of finally crossing this legal line and making her his in the eyes of the law, his family, and for the sake of their baby.

Rosie woke up the morning before the wedding with a sinking feeling in her chest and an overwhelming sense that something was wrong. It was a free-floating premonition of doom that didn't ease as the day went on and she was forced to endure a family lunch with her father, Melina, her mother and stepfather, and Aristotle at her side. The tension was thick enough to cut with a knife, and no matter how skilfully Aristotle managed the conversation to deflect any potentially fraught topics, to keep things civil, she was aware of the same anger and animosity her mother had always felt, targeted not only at her father, but also at Melina.

Rosie's defensive hackles were raised early on, and refused to settle. It was a relief when the lunch was finally over, and she was able to go home with Aristotle. But it was not for a leisurely afternoon. She'd had the bright idea of organising a hairdresser some time ago, to come and touch up her style a little, and a manicurist to attend to her nails. Both came to the apartment, yet it was still exhausting having to make conversation and play the part of the ebullient, excited bride.

Because as the day stretched on, and their wedding drew closer, she could only acknowledge that the sense of doom and uncertainty was growing, making it almost impossible to ignore.

Just get through it. You know this is the right decision.

But what if that wasn't the case? What if this instinct—demandingly persistent—was actually a smarter part of her brain finally kicking into gear before it was too late?

Marrying him was one thing, when it had just been about the baby. But what about herself? How would she do this, knowing that she loved him?

And she really did know that now. The realisation that had flooded her completely as they'd dined on Tharkos had only strengthened with every minute that they were together. And in fact, every minute they were apart, too. He had become a living, interwoven part of her, reminding her often of those ruins in Pompeii, and the tangled limbs of long-ago lovers.

But almost as if their child *knew* she needed the reminder of what they were doing and why, as Rosie walked the hairstylist to the door then locked it behind her, a fizzing feeling erupted in her tummy, like a small pop, and she gasped as she pressed a hand to it and laughed. All premonitions of doom were forgotten.

'Aristotle!' she called at the top of her voice, not daring to walk towards him lest the baby stop moving. 'Come here!'

He sprinted from wherever he'd been—his home office, she presumed—into the foyer. 'Are you okay?' His concern was obvious and she felt a rush of compunction for having worried him.

She smiled brightly. 'I'm fine, totally fine,' she reassured him, reaching out and grabbing his hand. 'The baby moved! I can *feel* the baby move.' She pressed his palm to her belly and moved her other hand beside it, laughing again as another backflip shifted and connected with the wall of her stomach.

He frowned, clearly concentrating. 'I don't feel it.'

'Ahh,' she groaned, sympathetic for him. 'I've read that it can take a little longer for someone else to feel, but it's incredible,' she said, eyes filling with tears. 'I thought… I mean, I know I'm pregnant, obviously. But this is the first time I've felt as though the baby is really inside of me, really a part of me. I can feel them. Their whole little self. Our baby. It's incredible,' she repeated, staring up at him, overcome by powerful emotions.

He stared back at her, moving his hand from her belly to her hip, his other joining it on the other side.

'*You're* incredible,' he corrected, and her pulse exploded as her whole chest seemed to crack wide open. Fireworks were dancing on the periphery of her mind.

'Aristotle,' she said, staring up at him with wonder and certainty. *I love you.* The words were there, at the front of her mind and on the tip of her tongue, but somehow, she held back from saying them.

He lifted his hands though, cupping her face, staring down at her with so much emotion in his eyes that everything lurched and tipped off-balance.

'I have something for you,' he said in a low voice, dropping his hands then, stepping backwards. 'A wedding present.'

Her insides twisted. 'Oh?'

'Come, sit down,' he said, guiding her through the apartment to the living room, which was considerably less sterile now she'd been let loose on it. Without asking his permission, she'd worked with Melina to bring some favourite items here from the mansion—a chair Rosie had always loved to read in, a clock that had sat in Aristotle's father's study, and some of the brighter, more modern paintings that were the perfect foil to his rigidly austere aesthetic.

He guided her not to the armchair, but rather to the dining table and she watched as he disappeared from the room. A few minutes later, he returned with a very large rectangular package.

'What is it?' she asked as he placed the gift down carefully on the table.

'Open it. Find out. But be careful—it's old.'

Her fingers were trembling slightly as she moved to unfasten the tape, and open the paper. She peeled the corners back slowly and then pushed the paper back completely to reveal the cover of a book.

The *Odyssey.*

It was incredibly old, bound in the finest leather, but she knew instantly what it was.

'Aristotle…' She could hardly speak. She didn't dare touch it without gloves. 'This is an original Chapman edition, isn't it?'

His eyes met hers, something in their depths like pride, or even affection, perhaps? 'Yes.'

'Oh my God,' she said, shaking her head. 'This is…incredible. Rare and…so generous.' And thoughtful. So incredibly thoughtful. Because he knew what the story meant to her. And yet, to gift her a book that was four hundred years old…

'It seemed appropriate,' he said, making her wonder if he understood the story, and knew the enduring theme was of lovers separated, being loyal to one another and fighting to be reunited. A story of great love and faithfulness, an epic for the ages.

'I love it,' she whispered, staring at it and wondering how quickly she could arrange appropriate storage. Something this old and valuable needed to be under preservation glass as much as possible.

'I have it arranged,' he said, so she glanced up at him sharply. 'The glass. I wanted you to be able to see and feel it first.'

She closed her eyes on a wave of emotion. It was the most touching thing anyone had ever done for her. She pushed her chair back from the table, standing on a tangle of feeling, as tears filled her eyes and she knew she needed some distance between splashes of salty water and the book.

'Thank you,' she choked out again. When she blinked at Aristotle, it was to find him watching her, in a way that made her whole body explode with certainty. 'I have to tell you something.'

Don't do it. Don't do it.

'Something you might not want to hear.'

It's going to change everything, and things are so good right now.

'But I think it's important for you to know, before we get married.'

He's going to freak out.

'The thing is, I've learned so much over the last month. About myself, but also about you.'

This is going to backfire.

But he was waiting patiently, eyes on her, clearly with no idea of the bomb she was about to throw into this perfectly calm life they'd established.

'You feel let down by the people who were supposed to love you.'

He stiffened visibly. She rushed on.

'Your parents—both biological and adoptive. One set

for giving you up, the other for lying to you about your birth. You have felt rejected and misled for as long as you've known about it, and it's completely changed how you approach life. Even though your adoptive parents clearly loved you with all their hearts, you stopped letting yourself love them a long time ago.'

'They are my parents,' he interrupted darkly. 'Of course I care about them.'

'You can't even say it.'

He scowled at her.

'It's like you stopped letting love of any kind in a long time ago.'

His nostrils flared. 'Why is this relevant?'

'Because you can't stop people from loving you. Your mother loves you; our baby is going to love you. Are you seriously going to refuse to admit you love them too?'

'Our child will know how valued they are, from the day they are born.'

'Do you think that's enough?'

'We're getting married tomorrow. Isn't it a little late to question me on this now?'

'It's not too late until the ink has dried on our marriage certificate,' she said, aware that this conversation was going in completely the wrong direction.

'What the hell are you saying, Rosemary? Are you having second thoughts?'

She opened her mouth to dispute that, but suddenly, she couldn't fight it any more. The sense of doom. The worry that if she married him, she'd be trapped. Trapped with a man who would torture her unknowingly, by failing to return her feelings.

'You know, four years ago, when we slept together, I made a mistake. I jumped to the wrong conclusion when I heard the awful things your friends were saying. Instead of giving you a chance to explain, and avoiding years of thinking I hated you, I could have just told you what I'd heard, and let you explain. But I didn't.'

He angled his jaw, regarding her without speaking. She knew it was the kind of look that would turn business rivals into jelly bones, because it was an innately disconcerting and intimidating expression, but Rosie was not so easily unsettled.

'I'm not going to make that mistake again.'

'What exactly are you trying to say?'

'That I love you.' She rushed the words out and without waiting for his reaction continued, 'And I don't want to marry you hiding that, presuming you'll never be able to love me back, when maybe, just maybe, knowing how I feel about you might let you accept that you are, in fact, worthy of love. Maybe you'll actually let me love you, and eventually—'

'No,' he interrupted before she could utter the secrets from deep within her heart. 'Don't keep saying this.'

It was a groan, as drawn from his heart as her last statement had been from hers.

'You are pregnant. That's a powerful biological impetus. It's natural that you would start to believe you feel something for the father of your baby, particularly given our living situation, and the fact we've been sharing a bed for weeks. It was careless and stupid of me to allow that to happen. We should never have confused sex with what we are.'

'But sex *is* a part of what we are—and it's so much more than that. It's making love, Aristotle. Surely you can see that? The connection we feel is so much more than physical.'

He swore sharply in his own tongue, the harshness of the word ricocheting around the room.

'Stop this,' he pleaded, stalking towards her and standing toe to toe, anguish in his face. 'You need to let this go.'

She bit down on her lip, to stop herself from sobbing. She'd told him because she wanted to learn the truth—and now she had it.

'Okay,' she said unevenly, taking a step backwards and feeling as if the whole world had shattered beyond recognition. 'If that's what you want.'

'What I want is to rewind ten minutes, and have this conversation not take place. Rosemary, what we share is good. It works. It is everything I want. But if you feel differently, if marrying me is going to make it hard for you, then we cannot go through with it.'

Her heart went into freefall as she stared across at him. 'I will not fight you for custody of our baby,' she said.

His eyes swept shut as his skin paled. 'I should never have threatened you with that. I was desperate. Panicked. I just needed to secure this future for our child. I have no intention of taking you to court, Rosemary, because I know, no matter what happens between us and how you feel about me, that you will be reasonable and fair.'

He was right. She'd never stop him from seeing their baby.

'I am staying at a hotel tonight,' he said, his voice coming to her as if from a long way away. 'I had planned to do so all along. Tradition, and all that,' he said, dragging a hand through his hair. 'You should use the night to think. Work out if you can do this. If you can't, we'll come up with a new plan tomorrow.'

'Another contract?'

'If necessary.'

She closed her eyes on a wave of pain. 'Okay. I'll think.'

But thinking when one's heart was splintering into a million pieces was no mean feat.

CHAPTER THIRTEEN

It really didn't occur to him that she might not show for the wedding. When he didn't hear from Rosemary, he'd simply presumed she'd thought things through and decided that her declarations of love had, after all, been born of her pregnant state. Wishful thinking. A need for connection that made no sense, given who they were.

But as he stood at the top of the family chapel, with the tiny group of family guests assembled, as well as the minister, and the clock ticked onwards, he began to realise the fatal flaw in his plan.

He'd left too much to chance. He'd demanded his own pragmatic approach to relationships. From the very beginning, he'd taken her at her word, that she wanted to avoid the sort of emotional situation that had led to her parents' miserable marriage and acrimonious split. When she'd *shown* him all along that she was a creature of passion, no matter how much she wished she wasn't. The kind of passion that was contagious, and had rubbed off on him. When they were together he felt it, too, like a livewire. A spark.

'Did you speak to her today?' his mother hissed audibly to Rosemary's father.

Glen shook his head once, frowning.

'I'll text her.'

He pretended not to notice as his mother pulled her phone from her bag and loaded up a message to send. More time passed. His gut twisted with something like concern and then, acceptance.

She wasn't coming.

He'd told her to think, and she'd made her decision as clear as the day outside.

And even though he'd told himself that things between them were businesslike and professional, it didn't matter. For the second time in his life, he felt that the rug had been pulled out from under him. That he'd lost something he hadn't realised he cared so much about keeping. Not Rosemary alone, but their whole life. Their child, their family.

Except, they weren't a family. No matter what she might say, this had all come about because of a mishap with her contraceptives. They weren't anything more than a cluster of fateful choices.

She wasn't coming.

The crunching of gravel sounded outside and something in his chest soared, halfway spearing him. His mother smiled as Glen stood up and strode towards the door.

'She's here!' he called needlessly, the relief in his tone mirrored on everyone's expression—even Rosemary's mother, who glanced at her husband and smiled with relief.

Aristotle didn't smile.

If anything, the soaring in his chest had turned into something else entirely. An oppressive weight.

A burden of responsibility—and an awareness that he was at the fork of another crossroads. Just like the one he'd found himself at with the news of her pregnancy, when he'd faced two choices, he now contemplated the same predicament.

Music began to play and a moment later, she appeared

before him in the doorway of the church. She was backlit by the afternoon sun, her father holding her arm. She looked like an angel brought down to earth. But it didn't matter that there was a halo of gold surrounding her, he knew her too well to misunderstand her body language. The lift of her shoulders, the ramrod straightness of her spine, the tilt of her chin.

With every single bone in her body, she was conveying a single message: *I'm strong. Bring it on.*

She was preparing herself for this wedding—their marriage.

She was braced for impact.

And he refused to let her.

He refused to let this be the case: for this to be her life.

He held fast as she walked towards him, conscious of the family members watching on—conscious of everything. The promises they'd spun like delicate spiders' webs as they planned for their baby's arrival, talked about their marriage. It would be so easy to reach up and strike his hand through those carefully crafted spools of hope—but then what?

'Rosemary…' he said as she approached. Up close, it was even worse. Her eyes barely glanced at his before skittering off to hide away from him.

Her father, none the wiser, smiled as though this was a wonderful dream come true.

For Rosemary, it was so clearly the opposite.

But the wheels had been set in motion. The playacting had begun.

Glen lifted Rosemary's veil and kissed her forehead. Aristotle's gut twisted with guilt.

The minister began to speak, and as he did so, Aristotle kept his gaze on Rosemary's face, trying to wordlessly communicate with her. To reassure her. Or to reassure himself, perhaps, that she was okay.

But when it came to the vows, the world seemed to stop spinning. Rosemary's voice was so quiet it was almost inaudible. He almost wished they'd stuck to an Orthodox wedding instead, in which there would be little need for speech.

'Did you say something, dear?' the minister quipped.

Rosemary glanced up at him, cheeks growing pink. She spoke again, this time more loudly. Clearly. She was fine. At least, she was for the first few sentences. *'To have and to hold, from this day forward. For better, for worse, for richer, for poorer.'* Fine.

But then, when she reached the second part of the vows, '*In sickness and in health, to love and to cherish*,' her voice hitched and her eyes lifted to his, her lips pulling downwards a little, as though she couldn't quite fathom what was happening. *'Till death do us part.'*

'This is my solemn vow,' the minister supplied.

She glanced up at him, stricken, then nodded, turning back to Aristotle quickly. *'This is my solemn vow.'*

And he believed her.

She loved him. God, but he wished she didn't. He wished she'd stuck to the contract they'd signed, that she was bound by the same determination as him to exist in this marriage—this life—without complications. But she wasn't.

Her heart was open and raw, vulnerable and exposed.

'And now, for the groom,' the minister continued, and began to feed Aristotle his lines.

Aristotle didn't repeat the first sentence. He just stared at Rosemary with the strangest sense that they were in the eye of a storm—that the whole world around them was a twister of some sort, but here they stood, in a weird, eerie void that had finally clarified everything for him.

He didn't love her, but he cared for Rosemary enough to spare her pain. To save her from herself. She was marrying him because she loved him. He had to set her free for that exact same reason. She loved him, and this marriage would destroy her, if he allowed it to proceed.

'We need a moment,' he said, natural authority in his tone as he glanced first to the minister then to the small group of guests. 'Please excuse us.'

Before Rosemary could say anything, he reached down and took her hand, drawing her with him towards the door of the chapel and out into the piercing sunlight. He barely registered it—his mind had its own brightness, a hyperclarity that dulled everything else.

'What are you doing?' Rosemary asked, looking up at him, so he only then became conscious of the way he was still holding her hand.

'Not here.' They were still too close to the chapel, and their families. He drew her with him to the garden at the side, and the shade of a large tree he'd used to climb, as a boy, before the world became so complicated.

'Everyone is waiting for us.'

'They can wait.' He lifted a hand to her cheek as his whole world splintered and fractured for the second time in his life. 'We need to talk.'

Rosie could hardly catch her breath. She'd been feeling like this all morning. Mired in a pervasive sense of panic, a feeling that she was on a juggernaut from which there was no escape. At the same time, she didn't want to escape. She just needed the wedding to be over, to be out on the other side, so she could pick up the threads of whatever her new life would look like.

As if to calm her, the baby kicked and she pressed a hand

to her stomach, feeling that little lifeform, taking strength from their presence alone.

'This isn't really the time,' she said.

'It has to be now.'

Her heart stammered. 'Why?'

'Because if we keep going through the motions, we'll be married, and that no longer seems like the right choice for us.'

Shock slammed into her like a fist, so she stumbled back infinitesimally.

'What?' Her voice emerged as a husky whisper.

That no longer seems like the right choice for us.

'You're in love with me,' he said, matter-of-factly. 'And I don't love you. Only a sadist would hold you to our original agreement under those terms.'

Her lips parted on an anguished exhalation of air. 'You said it was my choice.'

'I was wrong to leave it to you.'

'But—'

'If you love me, as you say you do, then you were never going to put yourself first. I have to do that for you.'

She shook her head, rejecting his statement. 'I want to do this.'

'Because in the back of your mind, you hope that marrying me will eventually lead me to love you. It won't.'

She felt as though she was going to be sick. 'How do you know?'

He closed his eyes then, as if on a wave of hurt. She wished there was somewhere to sit down. Her knees felt weak.

'Because I won't allow it to.'

Her pulse throbbed. All morning, she'd felt as though she were walking through a nightmare, preparing for a wedding to a man she loved fiercely, who didn't love her back. She'd known that was the reality. But hearing him say it so baldly, while she was wearing this dress, of all things, made her feel like the same naïve, gauche twenty-year-old she'd been the first night they'd slept together. She was just a fool, who'd let herself dream of something so much bigger than she deserved. To want a man who could never want her.

'I'm so stupid,' she said, shaking her head as a tear slid down her cheek.

'You are *not* stupid, *agápi*. Far from it.'

'What do you call this?' she disputed. 'I have fallen in love with someone who has made it his life's mission to never love. What is that, if not incredibly dim-witted?'

'I should have protected you better.'

'You tried. You did everything you could, Aristotle. This isn't your fault. It's just—'

But how could she explain? How could she make him understand that it hadn't really been a choice at all? She lifted her hands then, pressing them to his chest. A part of her wanted to relieve him of this burden by pretending it wasn't a big deal, that she'd get over him. But that wasn't fair to Aristotle. Deep down, inside his big, burly man body, with that veneer of arrogant ruthlessness, was the fifteen-year-old boy who'd had his world obliterated. That boy deserved to know that her love was authentic, and eternal.

'I will always love you,' she said simply. 'I think I always have.' Another tear slid down her cheek. 'And if you ever wonder why, think back to this conversation.' She sobbed softly.

'I'm breaking your heart,' he groaned, pulling her against him and holding her tight. 'I'm so sorry, Rosemary. Believe me, if I was capable of giving you what you want, I would. I would do anything not to hurt you like this.'

'I know,' she sobbed again, aware that her make-up and tears would be leaving marks on his crisp white shirt, and not caring. Because wrapped in his arms, against the warmth of his chest, everything felt—for a moment—as it needed to be. 'This isn't your fault.'

He stroked her back, his fingers moving up and down her spine, warm and comforting, so she closed her eyes and allowed herself to pretend this was real. But it wasn't, and lying to herself wasn't going to make this any better.

She glanced up at him, ignoring the familiar lurch of need at the sight of his stubbled chin. 'What do we do?'

'I'll deal with it.'

'I don't just mean the wedding,' she whispered. 'I mean, after that. We're still having a baby.'

His jaw stiffened. 'And my wishes are unchanged.'

Her eyes widened. Surely he wasn't still threatening to sue for custody?

'I want to be in their life,' he said. 'But you need to think about what that looks like.'

He was ceding all control to her. All the decisions. He was giving her the ability to shape their futures. What was that if not proof that he cared for her?

'I will never stop you from spending time with our child,' she said, dashing away her tears.

'I know.'

'I just can't think clearly right now.'

'Of course. We have time.'

She sobbed.

This was the end for them, and yet it was nothing like she'd imagined an end. This was nothing like her parents' awful arguments, that resonated around the house with the force of a supernova. This was mature and adult, a reasonable, calm, considerate conversation about what was best for her.

Because they were different to her parents? Or because he didn't love her enough to fight?

She strongly suspected the latter.

If he loved her, Aristotle Machairas would let nothing and no one stand in his way. Come hell or high water, he would fight and slay mythical creatures with his bare hands, to make her his.

She looked sideways, towards the incredible bougainvillea that always managed to take her breath away with its beauty. She wished she hadn't looked at it: the vine would forever remind her of this. Her bleak acceptance that she was deeply in love with someone who would never return those feelings.

'I guess we should go tell them.'

His hand on her back moved to her cheek. 'I'll do that. Why don't you go home, start putting this behind you.'

Home.

Where even was that?

She thought of all the changes she'd made to Aristotle's penthouse now with a sense of mortification. She'd been playacting this whole time. Pretending to be his actual fiancée, acting as though she had any right to be in his life. She'd got carried away so quickly. Swept up in their fake engagement, all because in her heart of hearts she'd known she wanted it to be real.

She bit into her lower lip. 'I don't know if I can.'

'What do you mean?'

'It's not home,' she said, shaking her head.

'Do you want to go back to England?'

She closed her eyes against that thought, too. *This* was

home. Here, at the estate, where she'd spent so many blissful school holidays. Where she'd first set eyes on Aristotle.

'I think I want to stay here,' she said, gesturing to the house in the distance, then looking back at him. 'Is that weird?'

He held her gaze for a beat, then shook his head once. 'I would be glad to think of you having my mother and your father on hand for support.' A muscle jerked in his jaw. 'But I am only a phone call away, if you need anything.'

She swallowed hard, nodding once. 'Thank you.'

They sounded like polite strangers. After everything they'd been through, and with what was on their horizon.

'I'll walk you to the house,' he offered, but she shook her head. Her heart was breaking; he was right about that. She was trying to hold it together by sheer force of will.

'No,' she whispered. 'I'd rather go alone. If you're happy to just explain everything to them,' she said, fidgeting with her fingers.

'Of course.'

He stared down at her for so long she thought he might kiss her. It felt just like any other moment they'd shared in the past: charged with passion and feeling, and urgent need. But he took a step backwards, showing more restraint than her.

'I'll call you tomorrow, to see how you are,' he murmured, and she nodded, because she knew it was about the baby, rather than her.

'Goodbye, Aristotle.'

He watched her walk to the house with a deep, throbbing ache that started in his gut but pulsed through his whole body. He felt like running after her, to hell with everything he'd just said, and pull her to him, kiss her until they both forgot all of this. Forgot everything.

He felt like going back in time and letting the wedding happen. Standing at the altar, it had felt so wrong to go through with it, yet watching her walk away was somehow so much worse.

He opened his mouth to call her name, but all he could see was her beautiful face, tear-streaked, her lips parted on a sob. Because of him.

It kept him silent, and held him still.

'Darling, you must eat something. For the baby,' Melina said gently, placing the tray of food on Rosie's bedside table.

She tried to force a smile but her mouth seemed to have lost the ability. She eyed the food warily. Melina was right. She couldn't live on tea and crackers indefinitely, but the thought of food turned her stomach.

'I'll try,' she promised.

Her stepmother had been incredible over the last four days. Rosie had curled up in the bed in the centre of the room she'd always used since her father's marriage to Melina, stripped down to her underwear, the wedding dress hanging like a bad dream on the closet door. Melina had wordlessly removed it, and within hours, her clothes from Aristotle's penthouse had appeared, and been unpacked silently by her stepmother.

On the first day, no one had tried to talk to her. They'd seemed to understand that she needed to be left alone, trying to glue her heart back together.

The day after, her father had come to gently try to make sense of things. He'd explained that her mother had left, but sent her love. Rosie had dismissed the statement for what it was: her father trying to make out that her mother had any hint of normal maternal feelings. Rosie had curved her hand over her stomach and silently promised her child that she would never treat them in the same cold manner.

Whenever she thought of Aristotle, it was as though her heart was being rolled over spikes. True to his word, he'd called the next day, but she didn't answer. She couldn't bear to hear his voice. Instead, she'd sent a quick text reassuring him that she was fine.

She did the same thing when he'd called the next day, and the next, and on this day, too.

'It's a beautiful morning out there. Your father and I are going to go for a walk; would you like to join us?'

Rosie reached out and broke a corner off the piece of the bread Melina had brought. 'No, thank you.'

Melina sighed softly and kissed Rosie's forehead. 'I love you, dear one. See you at lunchtime.'

Rosie lay down when her stepmother left, any attempt to eat forgotten, as she fell back into a fevered sleep, and dreamed of a time when Aristotle had been, oh, so briefly, hers.

CHAPTER FOURTEEN

NOT FOR ONE moment did he doubt that he'd done the right thing. His proposal to Rosemary had been a panicked knee-jerk reaction to her pregnancy and knowing he needed to be a part of his baby's life. He hadn't really considered any alternative. He hadn't, for even a moment, given any credence to her suggestion that they could make it work without being married.

But they would.

They had to.

He'd proposed and truly believed they'd be able to keep their marriage simple. Her own experience with marriage, having witnessed her parents' arguments, had made him overly confident. Stupidly so.

And as a result, she'd become collateral damage. The last thing he wanted.

He stayed away from his mother's home for a week. He tried to call Rosemary each day, but she never answered. Despite the fact she'd texted him afterwards, with the same few words, '*I'm fine. The baby's fine*', he still felt a strange need to hear her voice.

He'd become used to her.

The apartment had become used to her. The whole space had changed, and in myriad ways, everywhere he looked, were little fragments of her. From the artwork to the furnishings to the potted plants.

Two weeks after what would have been their wedding day, he went to his mother's house.

He'd been putting it off to give Rosemary time to get over what had happened, but fourteen days had seemed to stretch like an eternity, to the point where Aristotle could wait no longer. He needed to see her. To be sure she was okay. Despite what she said in her messages, it wasn't enough.

'Oh, darling!' Melina met him at the door, surprise obvious on her features. And with good reason. He rarely came home, yet he'd been multiple times in the last six weeks, because of Rosemary.

'Hello,' he greeted her with a kiss on her cheek.

'Come in, come in. I didn't know you were going to visit. Glen and I were about to go for a walk, but we can delay that. Would you like a coffee?'

He shook his head. 'I came to see Rosemary.'

Melina glanced over her shoulder, at Glen's arrival into the foyer.

He looked at Aristotle with a tightening in his features, a reaction of displeasure that he quickly smothered—and which made Aristotle feel strangely ashamed. Glen was judging Aristotle as the man who'd hurt his daughter, but the judgement was unnecessary. Aristotle judged himself plenty harshly enough. He knew what he'd done. He'd spent the last two weeks unable to get the image of Rosemary on what should have been their wedding day out of his mind. Her beautiful face, hair, that dress. Her vulnerability. Her willingness to marry him, even though she knew it would hurt her. Her courage and strength.

His eyes met Glen's—he was not a man to shy away

from criticism—but his throat felt oddly sore, as though he'd swallowed razorblades.

'Oh, darling,' his mother said, putting a hand on his forearm. 'I'll check with her, but...'

He swallowed quickly.

'She doesn't want to see anyone,' Glen's voice finished the sentence.

'Nonetheless, I shall go and ask. Come in, wait inside.'

'That's fine,' he said, pressing his hands into his jeans. He'd never felt more like an outsider. Strangely though, where as a younger man he'd felt jealous of the way his mother had taken Rosemary under her wing, and so clearly adored her, he now felt only glad. Rosemary and his mother deserved each other—they each deserved the love that he could no longer give.

He glanced away, hating the rush of emotions that was taking him hostage.

His mother disappeared inside, leaving Glen standing a few metres away in the foyer, and Aristotle on the doorstep.

At first, neither spoke.

Then, slowly, Aristotle turned to face the older man, expelling a long, deep breath. 'I didn't mean to hurt her.'

Glen just looked back at him, his eyes—so like Rosemary's—scraped over him, from his head to his toes and back again. Finally, he nodded once. 'I'm sure you didn't.'

It was more than Aristotle deserved, and somehow made him feel even worse. 'How is she?' His voice cracked slightly so he cleared his throat.

'Hard to say. She doesn't leave her room.'

Aristotle's gut dropped to his feet. 'What?'

Glen nodded once, to confirm what he'd already told Aristotle.

'It's been two weeks.'

He shrugged his shoulders. 'I don't know what you want me to say. She's devastated. But she'll get over it, eventually.'

His stomach rolled painfully. He felt an uncharacteristic need for support. To press his back to the rendered stone walls of the house, to hold himself upright. Two weeks, in her small bedroom.

Now he saw Rosemary as she'd been those last few weeks together, revelling in her impending motherhood, their upcoming wedding, in the exploration of her body each night with him, in the meals they'd shared, the stories she'd told about her various digs, her beautiful smile and laugh.

She was so gloriously unique, and he'd broken her.

What the hell was he doing here? Coming to the house as though he had any damned right to see her. As though he could assuage his conscience by seeing her and knowing that she was fine, when she clearly wasn't.

As if to underscore that, his mother returned a moment later and shook her head once, her eyes softened with sympathy. 'She'd prefer to be left alone for now, my love.'

Of course she would.

'Yes, I see,' he said, taking a step backwards, shoving a hand into his pocket. His heart dropping to his toes. 'Okay.' But he just stood there, staring straight ahead, processing this, missing Rosemary like hell. Craving just one glimpse of her, one small sighting. To hear her voice, even. 'Would you ask her to call me?'

His mother opened her mouth to say something, but then nodded. 'I'll ask her for you,' she said, without promising any success.

She didn't call him. Aristotle became obsessed with his phone, keeping it with him for the next two days, wherever he went. He wouldn't so much as shower without having the damned thing in sight. The most he received was the same pro forma text, telling him she was fine, the baby was fine.

A week after going to his mother's house, he'd reached his limit. He texted back:

You are not fine. Have you left your room yet?

She didn't reply. The razorblades feeling in his throat was back. So too the sense that his stomach had been hollowed out completely and then removed. He was both exhausted and restless, but his focus was shot to pieces. Work was barely worth contemplating.

If only he knew that she was okay, he'd move on. If he could just imagine her happy, going on with her life, exploring the mansion, walking freely over the estate as she had as a teenager, if he could only know that he hadn't made her so miserable…then he'd feel better. He'd feel normal, and he could start to put all this behind him.

A week after that, and he was at the end of his patience. This was getting ridiculous. This time, he texted his mother before leaving his place.

I'm coming over. Please tell Rosemary I expect to see her.

He didn't check his phone again, but when he arrived, he saw his mother had responded:

I don't think she's ready.

He ignored it. He was done being frozen out. He needed to see her like he needed to breathe.

He strode to the door and pressed the buzzer, waiting impatiently. A housemaid opened it inwards. He swept inside without waiting for an invitation, and stalked towards the stairs. He knew which room she was in, and if she wasn't going to speak to him, or tell him anything more about herself, he'd damn well go to her and…and…what?

He didn't know.

But not seeing her was killing him. Not talking to her was a form of torture.

At the door to her room, he lifted his fist and knocked swiftly. 'It's me, Rosemary.'

He heard a shuffle, a movement of a chair, perhaps, against the floorboards.

'I'm coming in.'

'No.'

Her denial came a second too late; he'd already pushed in the door and felt the bottom fall out of his world for the second time in a month. If he had been asked, a moment earlier, what Rosemary looked like, he would have been able to describe her in minute detail, and yet he looked at her now almost as if for the first time.

She was so beautiful, so incredibly striking, but there was such a hollowness to her that he couldn't see her without feeling the gravity of what he'd done. The hurt he'd wrought. He swore as he entered the room, striding across to her but stopping a foot away, when she flinched visibly and took a step backwards.

'Please, don't be here,' she said, shaking her head, her eyes huge in her face. Her face that looked…gaunt. Pale. His eyes swept over her more critically, studying her for changes, noting that while her stomach was rounder, the rest of her looked…slimmer. Was that possible in pregnancy? His gut swooped.

'You need to come home,' he said, crossing his arms over his chest, his heart thumping hard.

'I have no home.' Tears filled her eyes; she blinked them away. 'Please, Aristotle, leave. I'm not ready for this. I can't do it.'

'Fine. We don't have to do anything. But I cannot leave you here, if this is what happens.'

'What? If what happens?'

'You're losing weight. You look miserable.'

'I'm fine.'

'Stop saying that!' he shouted, but she shook her head, anger and frustration evident in her beautiful face.

'I'm not fine, okay? I'm not fine. But I will be. I just need time.'

'I'll give you time, but under my roof, where I can make sure you're eating, and doing things that make you happy. Not here.'

'Your mother is taking care of me.'

'You are literally fading away.'

'I'm really not.'

'Oh, Aristotle—' his mother appeared at the door, her eyes sweeping from her son to Rosemary '—I didn't realise you'd arrived. I thought I told you it wasn't a good time…'

He glared at her. 'Damn it, you should have told me this was happening to her.'

Melina glanced at Rosemary, her expression showing the concern she obviously felt. 'What good would that have done? You cannot fix this, Aristotle.'

'I broke it; of course I can fix it.'

'I'm not an "it",' Rosemary interjected. 'And your mother's right. I'm not your problem—'

'You are my…you are…'

'Yes?' Rosemary demanded, her eyes sparking with his. 'What am I?'

'The mother of my child,' he said, immediately shaking his head at how insufficient that seemed. His concern for her was not motivated purely by her pregnancy. It was bound up in Rosemary as a person, as the woman he'd become used to having in his life. The woman he loved to see smile.

'Please leave,' she whispered, confirming that she too felt he'd said possibly the worst thing he could have.

'Not without you.'

'Well, unless you're going to kidnap me,' she muttered, not realising that he would indeed stoop to that. To confirm it, he reached down and picked her up easily, cradling her against his chest.

She squawked and hit his shoulder. 'Put me down, you fool. This is absurd.'

'No, absurd is you being here, wasting away, when you should be at my home, where I can care for you.'

'Aristotle,' Melina hissed, 'you cannot behave like this. I don't know what's come over you. Honestly, to think my own flesh and blood could carry on like this—'

Now it was his mother who'd said the exact worst thing at the exact worst time. His patience was already stretched to breaking point.

'Just as well I am *not* your flesh and blood then, isn't it? You can put this behaviour down to my biological parents—whoever the hell they may be.' And he stalked out of the room with a now silent—shocked—Rosemary held tightly to his chest.

He'd made it to his car when Glen Richardson burst from the house like a man possessed. 'Just what the hell did you say to her?' he roared as his eyes swept over Aristotle and then Rosemary, who had stopped arguing, at least. But at the car he had no option to put her down, and the second he did, she stepped away from him, looking at him as though he was a lit fuse.

Control—something he valued almost above anything else—seemed totally out of his grip.

'Your mother is in there, looking like she's about to pass out, or vomit, or both. What did you say?'

He refused to soften. Refused to regret what he'd said.

'Something I should have said a long time ago.' He turned to Rosemary. 'Come with me.'

But it was a question. A plea. A need deep in his chest for her to be back in his home, where he was convinced she belonged.

She shook her head slowly, tears sliding down her cheeks. 'I can't.' But she came closer to him, lifting a hand to his cheek, cupping it gently. 'Are you okay?' Her voice trembled slightly, and her concern was almost his undoing. With anyone else, he would have been able to brush off the enquiry with some acerbic rejoinder. With Rosemary, it felt as though the truth was desperate to burst from him.

'Are you coming?'

She shook her head, her lips parting then closing. She swallowed, her throat visibly shifting with the movement. 'I can't. But you should go back in there, talk to your mum properly.'

He rejected that instantly. He hadn't meant to reveal what he knew to throw her concern back in Melina's face, but strangely, he didn't—couldn't—regret it.

'It's a conversation that we should have had a long time ago, and at her instigation. I am not interested in staying here to appease her conscience.'

He wanted to pull her with him. To lift her into the car and buckle her in, to take her back to his home and order all of her favourite foods. Somehow, he had a complete list in his mind of everything she'd eaten and loved in the past weeks. All of the things that had made her close her eyes and swoon as she'd tasted them. From octopus to lamb to prawn *kataifi* and chicken *souvlaki*. It was as though parts of his brain had rewired themselves completely, to become an expert on Rosemary Richardson.

Rosemary Machairas, his brain instantly supplied—the name he'd started to crave calling her. Strange, when it wasn't really even his name.

He wrenched open his car door and slid in behind the wheel, closing the door and putting down the window so he could regard Rosemary for another beat. 'You're sure?'

Her tears were still falling. It gutted him. 'Yes,' she whispered. 'If you're going, go.'

He didn't need to be told twice.

For the briefest moment, when his doorbell rang, his hopes soared. Every part of him burst with alertness, in the hope that he would open it and find Rosemary on the other side.

Of course, it was his mother. He wasn't remotely surprised. There was no way she could leave things the way they were, without an explanation.

'We need to talk,' she said, her lip quivering. Her eyes were red-rimmed, as though she too had been crying. So he was two for two then.

He stepped back and gestured into his home, though he was in no mood to have this out now. At least she was alone. Given the way Glen Richardson had looked like he wanted to pummel Aristotle, he wouldn't have been surprised if he'd accompanied Melina.

As she walked into the enormous living room her eyes

swept over it, clearly noting the changes, before she sat down on the edge of the sofa.

'How long have you known?'

'At least you didn't come here to deny it.'

She shook her head, face pinched. 'Oh, Ari.' She reverted to his childhood nickname, and something inside of him twisted painfully. Rejection of that, because it had all been a lie.

'How did you find out?'

He stiffened. 'Does it matter?'

She shook her head soulfully. 'I suppose not. When did you find out?'

'When I was fifteen.'

She swore then, dropping her head forward. 'I wish you'd come to us. This is not something you should have dealt with on your own.'

His nostrils flared. 'I spoke to him.'

'Your father?'

He nodded once, a curt shift of his head.

Melina's brow creased. 'What did he tell you?'

'Trying to get your story straight?'

Melina fixed him with a steady glare. Despite the pallor of her skin, there was strength and determination in her features. 'Do not speak to me like that, Aristotle Machairas. Whatever else you might think, I *am* your mother, and I raised you to be better than this.'

He flinched at her summation, aware that she was right. But if ever there was a time for some anger, this was it.

'He told me that I was adopted, that he had no idea who my birth parents were, and that there was no possible way of finding out. He told me that I should never bring it up with you, because it would devastate you. And that was the end of it.'

His mother's eyes were huge. She stared at him for several seconds before she stood tremulously and paced towards the piano, pressing a finger to the ivory keys without making a sound.

'That fool of a man,' she muttered, shaking her head. For the second time that afternoon, he watched as a woman's face became slippery with tears.

'Would you have preferred he deny it?'

She spun around to face him then, arms wrapped around her slender frame. 'Aristotle, Stavros *was* your father.'

He should have been used to the feeling of the earth tilting wildly beneath him, but he wasn't yet.

'What?'

She lifted a hand and fidgeted with the necklace she wore. He'd noticed, but never really comprehended, that she'd threaded her engagement ring around it—the one given to her by Stavros.

She pressed a hand to the piano, this time obviously for support.

Aristotle stood very, very still.

'You know I had a twin sister, darling?'

He frowned, unsure of where this was going, but nodding.

'She passed away, about a year before you were born. It was a very, very bad time in my life. She and I were soulmates, in so many ways. She was my other half. I didn't cope well with her loss. At the same time, your father and I had been struggling with fertility issues for almost two years. Honestly, I've never been in such a dark place.'

His frown deepened. He could easily believe that. His mother was nothing if not optimistic. She had a never-ending supply of practical, cheery advice for any situation.

'I ran away.'

He stared at her.

'I don't mean literally. I mean that I ran from my life. I thought if I went somewhere else, became someone else, I could escape the grief.' Her lips twisted in a hollow grimace. 'It didn't work.'

He nodded, clearing his throat, not sure what he could say. It didn't matter, anyway. His mother was unburdening herself.

'I didn't realise it, but in leaving your father, I put him through the worst time of his life, too. He was broken, Ari. Completely destroyed. I'd been carrying so much pain over not being able to conceive, I didn't realise that he had been experiencing the same thing. He was always so strong—so incredibly strong. He didn't let himself show his grief—he thought he had to support me.'

It was impossible not to hear this without feeling an ache, deep in his gut, for these people who'd raised him.

'In the time we were separated, he met someone else. It wasn't serious—they only saw each other a few nights. He was simply looking to forget, too. She fell pregnant, but didn't tell him. The first we knew about you was a few weeks after you were born.'

Aristotle felt as though he could barely breathe.

'She had been in a bad car accident. She almost died, but they were able to bring her into the hospital and keep her in a coma long enough to deliver you. We might still never have known, except she'd been preparing documents with a lawyer, and in those documents she'd specified your father's name as your next of kin, without identifying his paternity. But by the time we were notified, her name alone was on the birth certificate. To make you ours legally, we had to adopt you. Besides, your father didn't want to risk anyone else learning what he'd done.'

Aristotle's chest filled with the strength of his emotions. 'Why didn't he tell me any of this?'

'I suppose to protect me,' she said, but with evident irritation. 'I took it very hard, that I could not conceive. And yet, from the first moment I held you, I made you—and your poor late mother—a promise. There was no one else, Ari. She had no family, no siblings, no one to step in. So I swore I would love you with every fibre of my being. I would love you so utterly and completely as though you were my own, almost until you were sick of me.' Then she sobbed. 'My darling, I did. I have. I have held you in my heart, giving you all of the space there, because that is what you deserve.' She crossed to him then, putting her hands around his arms. 'Can you really say you have any shadow of a doubt as to how much I adore you?'

He closed his eyes on a growing wave of guilt. A feeling that he had spent all the time since he was fifteen pulling away from his parents—who had loved him, just as she said.

'He should have told me,' Aristotle said in a choked voice.

'Yes. But he wanted to protect me, you see. He loved me, from the first moment we met until his last breath, as I loved him. I know how hard you found it that I married again so quickly afterwards, but had it not been for the way your father stretched my heart, I don't know if I could ever have loved another man.' She sighed, shaking her head, her perceptive grey eyes lancing him thoughtfully. 'He should never have let you suffer like this though, all to spare my feelings. Only he loved me so much, every day we had together. Sadly, though, my darling, love can sometimes make you really, really stupid.'

CHAPTER FIFTEEN

It was only after she'd left that he let those words really sink in, and make sense. It was only after she'd left that he thought about love, and vulnerability, the great leap of faith that it took to love someone, and finally understood what, on some level, he'd known all along. Known, but chosen to determinedly ignore. Known, but resisted with every inch of himself, with every breath in his body, until the strain of pretending he didn't care was threatening to tear him to shreds.

Love could make you stupid.

Really, really stupid.

His curse tore through the apartment as he dragged a hand through his hair, staring out at the view, looking, this time, to the east, towards the mountain upon which his family's estate stood. More importantly, towards Rosemary. Almost as if by looking towards her, she might feel a difference in the atmosphere. Might understand the epiphany he'd had—that he should have been brave enough to understand, months before this. Years?

He cursed again, but this time it was accompanied by a swift movement as he crossed through the penthouse towards the front door, grabbing his keys from the console table as he swept by. Having recognised what was in his heart, he couldn't go another moment without acting. He just hoped it wasn't too late.

For almost the first time since their abandoned wedding, Rosie left her room. It was a beautiful late summer's day and the garden was in full bloom. Fragrant and evocative of so many of her best memories. Confident that she could still be left alone out here, she chose to walk amongst the citrus grove, lined as it was by the most fragrant hedge of gardenias. She breathed them in as she went, aware that if she were to reach out and touch the velvety white flowers they would turn brown by the morning.

She did allow herself to pick one, though, plucking it carefully from its hedge and holding it to her lips, closing her eyes as she inhaled that sweet vanilla scent.

When she heard gravel crunching underfoot, coming from behind her, she presumed it would be her father, intent on bringing her back for dinner. She knew they were worried about her, and she felt terrible about that. It hadn't been her intention to cause them any concern. She just knew she needed space and time to heal. Maybe it was working.

Or maybe it was just that seeing Aristotle today had put a temporary plaster over her heart, giving her the false hope that the emotional torment was almost at an end.

She angled her face, only half turning. 'I'll come in soon, Dad. I just want to see the sunset.'

He didn't answer. She stopped walking then, sighed softly and turned around, schooling her features into a mask of contentment, even when she didn't feel it.

But the mask slipped the second she saw Aristotle standing only a few feet behind her, wearing the same suit he'd been wearing earlier. And yet, somehow, he looked different.

‘Aristotle…’ She could hardly say his name. She wasn’t ready for this. ‘What are you doing here?’

‘I came to see you.’

She closed her eyes as the summer breeze lifted the magnolia scent and carried it towards her.

‘We’ve already seen each other.’

‘Fine—I came to talk to you.’

‘We’ve done that, too.’

‘Not really.’

She blinked across at him, frowning. ‘Is there something else you have to say?’

‘Yes, in fact. A hell of a lot.’

She shook her head, rejecting that, but her feet didn’t move and nor did her lips. She could only stare at him beseechingly.

Finally, in a last-ditch effort at self-preservation, she murmured, ‘Please, Aristotle. Leaving you almost destroyed me. Don’t make me go through any more. I just can’t bear it.’

‘I spoke to my mother,’ he said pensively, eyes raking her face.

She wished she didn’t care, but how could she not? This affected two people she loved. Her curiosity was natural.

‘And?’

Her heart thundered as he explained the truth, tears filling her eyes. She shook her head on a wave of mixed emotions. Sympathy and compassion, anger and disbelief. How could Stavros Machairas have invented an adoption rather than admit to an affair? Particularly when, technically, he and Melina had been separated at the time.

‘I can’t believe he put you through that,’ she muttered, lifting a hand to drag a windswept lock of hair behind her ear, right as he went to do the same thing. Their fingers brushed and her whole body sparked with electric charge.

She dropped her hand quickly to her side, squeezing her fingers into her palm.

'I can.' His voice was gruff. 'He loved my mother enough to do anything for her.'

Rosemary frowned, glancing towards the horizon.

'Ever since he told me I was adopted I have felt this chasm of emptiness in my chest, a sense that I had been scraped hollow and was just an outline of a man.'

She shook her head. 'How can you say that? You, of all people. You are dynamic and real—a powerhouse. You walk into a room and the air seems to change. It doesn't matter where you come from, who your parents are, *you* are *you*.'

A muscle jerked in his jaw. 'The thing is, you're right. When my mother told me the truth I didn't feel a sense of closure—the healing—I might have expected. I didn't realise it, but that hole inside of me had already been filled.' His eyes bored into hers, the emotion in them taking her breath away. 'By you, Rosemary. By you, and our baby, and the life we built together.'

Her throat felt raw. Everything hurt. Tears flooded her eyes as she shook her head.

'I know we were happy,' she whispered. 'It would have been enough for me, you know. To marry you and live that life, even knowing you didn't love me and never would.'

'But it would never have been enough for me. Love can make you stupid, *agápi mou*, and I have been the worst kind of fool. Ever since I met you, I found you fascinating, but it wasn't until our parents' wedding, when I heard how my one-time friends were talking about you, that I realised I would set the whole world on fire before I'd let anyone hurt you.' A tear slid down her cheek. 'That night terrified me.'

'Why?' she demanded fiercely.

'Because I had become very good at keeping people at

a distance, but with you, I already felt you were under my skin. I couldn't get you out of my mind afterwards.'

She blinked quickly in an attempt to clear her tears.

'And then, at my mother's birthday party, I had prepared myself for seeing you, but that didn't stop me dragging you into my arms the first chance I got.'

'I didn't exactly fight you.'

His lips twisted in a grim half-smile. 'I have been fighting this for so long that I didn't stop to ask myself exactly *what* I was fighting.'

'Which is?'

'Isn't it obvious? I'm completely in love with you. I probably always have been. There is not a single doubt in my mind that this baby was gifted to us to make sure I wasn't so stupid that I let you go. Even on our wedding day, all I could think about was what would be right for you. I loved you so much, but not knowing that, I thought letting you leave would ensure your happiness. I've never felt so incredibly stupid. To think that I ruined everything, put you through this pain—put us both through it—believe me, Rosemary, I have been tortured by this separation as well. I have ached for you, needed you, dreamed of your smile and laugh. All I want, the hope that is deepest in my heart, is that we can start again—this time, understanding that we are together because of love.'

She sobbed again.

'I want to see the world with you, through your eyes, marvelling at the sites you love. When you go to a dig, our baby and I will come, to be near you, so you can work, and we can be together. I—' His brow furrowed and the light in his eyes dimmed. '*Christós*, I'm going too fast.' He took in a deep breath. 'I love you,' he said simply. 'Let me ask, before we think about the future, if you can find it in your heart to give me a second chance?'

'Aristotle...' she whispered, her heart beating so fast it was causing an actual painful fluttering in her chest. She lifted a hand, pressed it there, trying to calm it. 'If this is because you're worried about me, please don't.'

He opened his mouth to say something, but she lifted a finger and pressed it to his lips, needing to get this out.

'I've been to a lot of dig sites. I've studied a lot of ancient cultures. And there's one thing that always strikes me—the enduring familiarity of human emotions. The need to survive, to love, to grow—a need to feel safe.' Her hand dropped to his chest. 'Love is a part of life, so too is loss. And yet, the survivors move on.' Her eyes narrowed. 'I'm a survivor. This, right now, feels impossible, but I'm stronger than you think.' Her hand pressed to her stomach, feeling their baby in a way that gave her strength. 'We'll be okay.'

'I know that,' he said urgently. 'But I'm not so sure I will be. Particularly not if I have to face the future without the woman I love by my side, knowing it is all my fault.'

'You told me not to fall in love with you,' she reminded him. 'At every step of the way, you were honest with me.'

'No,' he denied instantly, moving to capture her hands in his and lift them between their chests. '*You* were honest with *me*. You were brave and saw the truth in your heart, while I ran from it like a coward. I don't want to run any more. I want to love you, for the rest of my life, Rosemary. Not for the baby, but for you. You have no idea how badly I want to bring you home with me and simply revel in having you there. In being able to see you, touch you, wake up next to you, share meals with you, hear you laugh. It is *you* I want. *You* I am obsessed with.'

She gasped, sucking in a sharp breath as his words unfolded inside of her.

'I have missed you,' he said, dropping his forehead and pressing it to hers. 'So much more than I can ever put into words.'

She bit into her lip, completely understanding.

'But if you let me, I will spend a lifetime trying. I will spend every day we are gifted together showing you how much you mean to me.'

'Oh, Aristotle,' she murmured, lifting a hand and cupping his stubbled cheek. 'Has anyone ever told you you're a very skilled negotiator?'

He was silent, as if uncertain whether that was the affirmative answer he so obviously needed. She tilted her face then, shifting their brows from connecting, moving so her lips brushed his.

'I love you,' she murmured against them. 'I didn't mean it like a teenage crush, though I've felt that for you, too. When I told you I love you, I meant it like this—real, forever, life-changing love. You are a part of me, Aristotle Machairas, and you have been for a long, long time. That's not going anywhere.'

'And nor am I.' He hesitated in an uncharacteristic act of uncertainty. 'Will you come home with me?'

She tilted her head to the side, pretending to consider that. But Aristotle, clearly still feeling as though he was running over quicksand, shook his head and swallowed a curse.

He knelt then, holding her hands in front of him, pressing a kiss to her fingers. 'I love you, Rosemary Richardson. You are deep inside my heart; all the goodness and light in my being comes from having known you and now, being free to love you. I didn't understand the truth of this when I suggested we get married—'

'Suggested?' she interrupted through tearful laughter.

'Okay, arranged.'

She laughed again. 'Sure, we'll go with that.'

'But even then, I knew I couldn't let you go again. I had been craving you in a way that had felled me to my knees. The baby was a chance to have you in my life. But it was always about you, and me, and this.' He shifted their joined hands to his chest, tapping near his heart. 'I love you, and nothing would make me happier than if you would agree to marry me for real. Not because you have any hint of fear in your heart, but because you know I am your other half, as much as you are mine.'

She waited just as long as she could. After all, it had been a long month of missing him; he could handle a few moments more of emotional torture. But only a few moments. And then, she was dropping to her knees and wrapping her arms around his waist.

'You are my everything,' she said. 'Of course I'll marry you.'

The paperwork was all in place, and for a somewhat exorbitant fee, the minister managed to clear his schedule for the following afternoon. Rosie's mother returned, though not without a few muttered complaints about the last abandoned wedding.

Rosie didn't care. She practically floated on cloud nine as she walked down the aisle of the Machairas family chapel towards her groom, and her destiny. There was not a hint of uncertainty, a smudge of doubt that this was right for her, and them.

He was her everything.

He was her future.

And one day someone would look back on this time, on

their ancient past, and learn the lessons of life and love from Rosemary and Aristotle's example.

On the day their baby was born—two weeks early, demonstrating their father's determined impatience—Rosemary was consulting on a small dig on the outskirts of Athens. No physical exertion was involved; she was simply providing advice on techniques and storage options at the very start of the project. Which wasn't to say she wasn't practically salivating at the thought of being involved, down the track.

The only saving grace was that her waters hadn't broken in the middle of the meeting. Instead, she'd felt the sharpening of a vague discomfort she'd known since morning, and as the conversation continued, the pains had grown more intense and come more quickly together, so towards the end she let out a small wince and groan.

'You're in labour,' a woman about ten years her senior said, putting a hand on her forearm. Then, to the team, 'She's having the baby!'

'Here?' One of the older archaeologists leading the research looked askance.

'Not if I can help it,' Rosemary muttered, pulling her phone from her bag and typing a quick message to Aristotle:

I'm in labour

'I'll take you to the hospital,' the same woman offered.

'I have a car, thank you.'

'Let me help you to it.'

As the sleek chauffeur-driven Machairas limousine pulled into traffic, Rosie ran a hand over her stomach and smiled serenely. While their baby's sense of timing might have been all Aristotle, their love of history was clearly her.

* * *

A bouncing Machairas baby boy entered the world with an indignant scream and a hefty nine-and-a-half-pound frame right on dusk. Strange, in a way, that as the brightness of the day faded, all the light burst fully into Aristotle and Rosie's world. Aristotle, who'd been by Rosie's side the entire time, was as overwhelmed by love for their child as she was.

Their family, in the waiting room, could scarcely wait to see this new addition, and as soon as Rosie gave the signal, Glen, Melina and Rosie's mother and stepfather came quickly into the room.

They named him Telemachus—Mack—Machairas after Telemachus of the *Odyssey.* How could they not? It was a story which held so much significance for both of them—Aristotle had long since realised that hearing Rosemary talk about reading the *Odyssey* was perhaps the first moment he'd started, deep down, to suspect that he loved her, and could never let her go. For Rosemary, Aristotle's incredible gift of the ancient copy of the book had forced her to admit her feelings. But more than that, Telemachus was an instrument for bringing his parents back together, a force that allowed their love to thrive. Though their love was now so much bigger than their son, they couldn't deny the valuable part he'd played in bringing them together.

Rosie had thought she might miss travelling and working on digs, but she became such a respected figure in the Greek archaeological community that there was no shortage of work in the country she was offered, and these were easy enough to travel to with her husband and son, or to commute.

They hated to be apart, and avoided it wherever possible.

It was little wonder that only two years after Mack's hasty arrival, a daughter was born—Anastasia, named for

Aristotle's birth mother. She was a part of him, after all. Though his father had made it all so much more difficult than it needed to be, Aristotle understood. He would also move heaven and earth to protect the woman he loved.

It was Melina, in the end, who'd helped uncover details of his birth mother's past, to learn at least enough about her to start to form a fuller picture of who he was and where he came from. Ultimately, though, while the information was important for him to have, nothing made him feel more complete, more whole, than the love of his wife and children.

He was grateful every day for the fact that Rosemary's father had taken a job at their estate, and come into their lives. With him, he'd brought Rosemary, like a breath of fresh air, the promise of his future, the anchor point for any stormy sea he might face.

His destiny, his love, his heart, for all time.

* * * * *